SERIES SILVER SERIES

SUPERB WRITING
TO FIRE THE IMAGINATION

Judy Allen says, 'For me, writing is not so much creating a new world as trying to understand this one – wondering what is behind or under things, wondering whether there are forces we know nothing about but which are as powerful and relentless as gravity or the struggle for life. In my stories the place becomes as important as any character – in fact it *is* one of the characters.'

Her *AWAITING DEVELOPMENTS* won the Whitbread Award and the Friends of the Earth Earthworm Award. Author of more than 50 books including *THE SPRING ON THE MOUNTAIN, THE STONES OF THE MOON, THE DREAM THING* and *BETWEEN THE MOON AND THE ROCK*, she also writes for radio.

THE BURNING

JUDY ALLEN

*Hodder
Children's
Books*

a division of Hodder Headline

To D. S.

First published in Great Britain in 2000
by Hodder Children's Books

A Catalogue record for this book is available from
the British Library

ISBN 0 340 73991 6

Typeset by Avon Dataset Ltd, Bidford-on-Avon, Warks

Printed and bound in Great Britain by
The Guernsey Press Co. Ltd, Channel Isles

Hodder Children's Books
A Division of Hodder Headline
338 Euston Road
London NW1 3BH

ONE

Imagine a house as a head. If it has windows for eyes, a door for a mouth, and walls which have ears, then the people who live in the house are the thoughts which move in the head.

If a house is a head, and the people in it are thoughts, then the people who have gone away are memories. And people, like thoughts, almost never go away completely – there's almost always something that remains – an echo of past emotion, a faint charge of energy, the sense that someone has just left an empty room, or is just about to walk into it.

And the subconscious of the house, where the hidden things are, is in the cellar, or in the spaces under the floorboards, or in the cavities between inner and outer walls, or up among the roof rafters.

Whatever lies buried in the sub-conscious may sleep for one or a thousand years, or even for ever. Or it may not. Something may disturb it, and once disturbed it may begin to stir, to move – slowly and blindly at first but relentlessly – up towards the surface . . .

The sound of the motorbike came first and then the bike itself followed. It kept up a good speed through the dark streets of the straggling town, but the rider slowed as he approached The Green, which was the heart of the village. The town had grown outwards and joined up with it years before. A traveller going in the opposite direction would find it hard to tell where the village ended and the town began, but the rider approaching The Green could see at once where the town ended and the village began.

He braked and stood still for a moment, his feet on the ground either side of the bike. At this hour there was no traffic. Everyone had already arrived home, first from school and later from work, and few had gone out again that evening.

He lifted his feet back on to the pedals and made a slow circuit, anticlockwise, around the long rectangle of The Green. As he passed, he glanced at the little row of terraced cottages, their front gardens full of the dead sticks and tattered brown leaves of November. He noticed the cottages that had been converted into shops – a newsagent, a greengrocer, a gift shop. He noticed the name of the gift shop – The Witches Cauldron.

If it had been daytime he might have noticed the small pile of wood in the centre of The Green. In the dark, though, with the light from the street lamps barely reaching it, it just looked like a shadow.

Beyond The Weaver's Arms public house, he turned left, along the top of The Green, and then drifted slowly down its other side. He passed the oddly misshapen chestnut tree; the church of St Mary's with the strange dark staining on its west wall; the Memorial Garden; the entrance to Mill Street.

As he passed, his reflection glinted in the windows of the shops, the houses, the pub. No one chanced to look out as he made that first circuit. Only the empty windows watched.

There was nothing about the sight of a motorcyclist to arouse memories in an ancient cottage. Or almost nothing. The machine was unfamiliar, the leathers and the helmet were strange. But the rider wasn't wearing his gauntlets, and his hands on the handlebars – thin hands with long fingers and a modest signet ring with entwined initials – were like other hands, hands of long ago, dead hands reborn.

He turned left again, along the bottom of The Green where the mini-roundabout linked Green Road with West Street, the road from town, and then began to circle The Green a second time.

Again his image slithered across an old cottage window, again the thin white hands were reflected briefly on the glass, and somewhere inside, in a dark quiet place, the smallest imaginable tremor moved the air. It was not like a full awakening. Not yet. But something that had lain in such deep peace that it might almost not have existed was now a little nearer the surface than it had been, just moments before.

TWO

The motorbike was not quite the only piece of traffic to disturb the quiet of that evening. A small van put in a brief appearance, to deliver a bundle of local papers to the newsagent. The newsagent grumbled, as usual, about always being the last port of call on the van's route, so that he had to stay open late. The driver shrugged, as usual, and the van moved off.

The local paper, written from Monday through Wednesday, printed on Thursday, published on Friday, mostly sold on Saturday and Sunday, carried a short report at the foot of its front page. The headline wouldn't have made sense to anyone who didn't already know what it meant. It read: NO TO GREEN FIRE.

NO TO GREEN FIRE

Once again, local residents are agreed The Green is not a suitable site for a bonfire on November 5th. Earlier this week a few pieces of old wood were stacked near the middle of this ancient and attractive grassy expanse, but were immediately removed by outraged householders. The voluntary ban on bonfires, which has stood for so very many years, is as strongly supported as ever.

It wasn't the local paper's fault, but it was a little out of date. The small pile of wood which had appeared on The Green on Tuesday, and been removed on Wednesday,

4

was replaced on Thursday and added to on Friday. It still wasn't much bigger than a boy scouts' camp fire. But it was growing.

THREE

The rider was circling what appeared to be an empty village. But several people heard the sound of the engine, and one or two glanced idly out.

The newsagent, closing the shop, wondered if he might be shutting out a potential customer, but decided he probably wasn't.

Cal, looking out from one of the top floor flats in the block in Mill Street, felt envy and resentment. The only bike he'd ever ridden had been stolen, and the owner had reclaimed it almost at once.

Gina, struggling with the shop accounts in the upstairs office, under the thatch in The Witches Cauldron, watched the bike make its third circuit, and frowned at the distraction.

Jan, on the phone in one of the terraced cottages, the one near the end, the one that was larger than those on either side of it, pulled the curtain back in time to see the tail light disappearing up Green Road. She was talking to Kate, who lived in one of the second-floor flats in Mill Street. It was three hours since the two of them had walked home from school together, and they were ready for their next conversation.

Jan mentioned the stranger orbiting The Green, so Kate carried the phone to the window and saw him, too.

Not that he was riding by that time. He'd parked the

6

bike and was wandering up Mill Street on foot.

'I can't see him any more,' said Jan. 'Has he gone?'

'No,' said Kate, pressing her forehead to the window glass. 'He's down here.'

Mill Street was a cul-de-sac, the whole of one side taken up by the enormous block of flats where Kate lived, the other by a line of modern 'executive' houses. Because it was a dead end, people turning into Mill Street were always heading for one of the flats or one of the houses. So each time he disappeared into the dark places between the street lamps, Kate assumed he'd gone in somewhere, but each time he reappeared. Up one side of the street he went, down the other, then back again.

'He's behaving very strangely,' she said. 'I think he's a prowler.'

'He's lost,' said Jan. 'A lost courier looking for a delivery address.'

'He isn't carrying anything, apart from the helmet, so he isn't delivering anything. And he isn't lost because he isn't nervous.'

'How can you tell?'

'It's cold – I can see his breath. He's breathing calmly.'

'He wouldn't have to get hysterical just because he's lost!' said Jan. 'What's he look like?'

'It's hard to see from up here,' said Kate. 'Hey – you know how the houses opposite go in pairs with an alley between?'

'Yes.'

'He's looking over the gates into the alleys.'

'He's lost his dog,' said Jan with conviction.

'He wouldn't have a dog on a motorbike! Oh – now he's going – towards The Green – he's putting on his helmet – the bike must be really close.'

'So what are we going to do this weekend, then?' said Jan, losing interest.

'Your turn to choose.'

'You think of better things to do. You choose.'

'You are so lazy, Jan,' said Kate. 'You are terminally lazy. O.K., well first of all it's my turn to do the laundry. And Dad says if I don't tidy my stuff out of the front room, one of us is going to have to leave home.'

'What do you mean?'

'He says there isn't room for two human life forms as well as all my junk. I think it's possible he has a point.'

'That'll only take a couple of hours. Won't it?'

'And you and I have an English assignment . . .'

'That might take longer! But not the whole weekend.'

'OK, we could go skating – rent a video – go up to the Mall, see who's around. Or we could be really controversial and help build the bonfire.'

'My Dad's decided to go for it,' said Jan. 'He says there's stuff in the attic we could burn, if Grandpa doesn't mind.'

'Why should he mind?' said Kate. 'It isn't his attic any more, is it?'

'No but if there's stuff in it, he must have put it there. He's only got a bedsitter in the sheltered place – he couldn't take much with him.'

'Right, let's go with the bonfire, then. So when do we raid the attic?'

'I don't mind. Whenever.'

'It was so much easier when we were neighbours.'

'We are neighbours.'

'I mean close neighbours,' said Kate.

Jan began to laugh. 'We are close neighbours!'

'Aargh!' said Kate. '*Closer* neighbours, then. You are so annoying, you know what I mean, I mean when you lived in the flat upstairs.'

'I'm only the other side of The Green now,' said Jan. 'I can see the end of your block from here. Ugh, I can see Cal. He's just come out.'

'Forget Cal,' said Kate wearily, 'He's never done anything to you.'

'He says horrible things.'

'It's only words,' said Kate. 'Tell you what, meet me on the corner tomorrow, usual time. I want to begin the essay now. They always take longer than I think.'

She heard the bike start, just past the end of Mill Street. A few seconds later Jan heard it roar past at speed and head off up the road to town.

Within five minutes, they'd both forgotten all about it. If he was a prowler, it seemed he'd done his prowling and gone. It didn't occur to either of them that he might come back.

In one of the attics, high under the thatch of the row of old cottages, the faint tremor that had disturbed the dusty air subsided. But it didn't fade away. It might be weak, uncertain, insubstantial – but something had quickened it, made it restive. It couldn't slip back into easy oblivion – not now, not again.

FOUR

A small, loose-leaf ring-binder, A3 size, dark green, less than half full, several days between each diary entry:

Nov 3.

Kate's working on her English assignment tonight. I can't be bothered. I've just let Marvin out of his cage and he's running all over my desk. I've made a wall of books so he can't fall off. I now have hamster hairs all over this page. It looks like there will be a bonfire on Monday night. Unless the objectors chuck water on it. Or unless it rains. Mum says it's not worth all the argument and fuss for a couple of hours of baked potatoes and sparklers. Dad says it'll be a street party. He says it'll help everyone leave the past behind. Mum says it'll stir the past up. I don't care either way. If they don't light this one Kate and I can go in to town to the big one in Central Gardens.

FIVE

There was no rain on Saturday morning, but there were restless clouds, high in the sky, and sudden cold flurries of wind that took all the loose leaves off the trees and spun them in the air before letting them fall.

Unlike the evening before, the village was active this morning, though the only person actually on The Green was the landlord from The Weaver's Arms exercising his dog. A few people were shopping locally, the rest were backing out their cars or walking up to West Street to catch the bus, heading for the supermarkets and other shopping opportunities in town.

As usual, people talked, in the shops, on the pavements, at the bus stop. Today, the conversations were mostly about memories. Or, rather, memories of memories – stories that had been passed down through families. No one still alive was old enough to have a personal memory of The Fire, though most people still spoke the words as if they formed a proper name, with initial capitals. It had been enormous, The Fire. It was said it could be seen from hundreds of miles away – or fifty – or anyway at least thirty.

Some of the scars were still clearly visible – the scorch marks seared into the west wall of the church – the wounded tree, half eaten by flames when it was young.

Some of the scars were hidden – the clear glass in the west window of St Mary's replacing the stained glass which had shattered in the intense heat – the Memorial Garden, planted on the site of the cottages which had been incinerated in minutes, many with their occupants still inside.

But whether the signs were obvious or hidden, they were not forgotten. There hadn't been a bonfire on The Green since The Fire, and there were several who believed there still shouldn't be.

Yet the pile of wood was gently growing and, with less than forty-eight hours to go now, decisions had to be made. Was it really such a dreadful thing to want a party? Would it really be an insult to the memory of lives lost, families trapped and destroyed by flames? Would the very stones of the church protest? Or would they understand that time had moved on; would they accept that it was better for the younger ones to enjoy a few fireworks close to home rather than wander off elsewhere and perhaps get into trouble? After all, none of the people who had suffered by The Fire were still alive. Even the injured and bereaved were long gone, into dust and memories, living on only in the genes of their descendants.

As recently as last year, a bonfire would have been unthinkable. This year, things were not so clear.

Jan and Kate, shuddering in the cold wind on the corner of Mill Street, still unable to decide how to spend the morning, couldn't help but pick up some of the agitation of indecision that hung on the air.

Agitation creates its own kind of energy, and the energy was infectious. If the thing that was half shimmering awake, deep in the subconscious of one of the cottages, needed some kind of power to fuel it, then

12

power was certainly available now. Perhaps there was even enough to enable it to begin to remember past skills, to test itself, to send the first fragile threads of influence out of its dark hiding place.

Possibly one of the threads found its way into the dreams of the black cat that lay sleeping on the low wall in front of the Memorial Garden.

Or possibly the cat was simply startled by the bike.

The bike came roaring down West Street with a suddenness that was almost threatening. It took the mini-roundabout fast and at an angle, and swooped on along the church side of Green Road. Jan, who was nearest the edge of the pavement, felt the heat of the engine as it passed.

At the same moment, something made the cat spring awake and race across the road towards The Green, head down, ears flattened.

Jan put her hands up to her face. Kate screamed. The biker wrenched the handlebars and hit the brakes.

The engine made a sickening choking noise. The bike tipped and threw the rider off and away, on to the road. His helmet clanged as he landed. The bike slid onwards, on its side, with a harsh grating sound, until it hit the trunk of the chestnut tree and lay still, bleeding tiny drops of black oil on to the grass.

The cat, untouched, stood staring for a moment. Then it padded across The Green in the direction of The Witches Cauldron.

SIX

When the bike crashed, Mr Walsh was sitting in his car with the engine running, and Mrs Walsh was on her way out of their cottage. He shut off the engine and ran, abandoning the car with the drivers' door wide open. She slammed the cottage door behind her and followed as fast as she could.

Jason from the greengrocers ran too. He was closer because he'd just dumped a stack of broken fruit crates on to the growing pile of wood in the centre of The Green. But The Green was wide, and for several seconds Jan and Kate were alone with the accident.

Kate gripped Jan's arm. 'It's him,' she hissed. 'It's the biker from last night.'

Together, shakily, they walked towards the figure lying in the road. As they reached him, he rolled over on to his hands and knees and then, slowly, stood up.

'Are you all right?' said Kate.

He didn't answer. As the Walshes and Jason gathered around him, he pulled off his leather gauntlets, slowly, carefully, and stretched out his fingers. Then he unbuckled his helmet and lifted it off.

'Careful!' said Mr Walsh sharply, as if he was afraid the head might come away with the helmet.

'I'm OK,' said the rider.

'Should we call an ambulance?' said Mrs Walsh, shivering with shock.

'I'm OK,' he said again. He passed his hand across his face and glanced down at himself, as if checking this was true.

'You were lucky, mate,' said Jason. He winked at the girls and loped back across The Green to the shop, leaving Jan blushing and Kate grinning.

'You *are* lucky,' said Mr Walsh, suddenly angry, glowering at the motorbike. 'You could have been killed or maimed. It's asking for trouble, riding a thing like that when you can't control it.'

'It wasn't his fault,' said Kate indignantly. 'A cat ran in front of him and he swerved to save it.'

'Well I didn't see any cat,' said Mr Walsh.

'There was a cat,' said Jan. 'The one from the Gift Shop. It's gone back over there.' She wiped her eyes on her sleeve. Something – probably the chill wind – was making them water.

'Doing stupid tricks, more likely,' said Mr Walsh.

The rider took no notice of any of them. He limped over to his bike and stood looking down at it.

'We're obviously not needed here,' said Mr Walsh. He cupped his hand under his wife's elbow and drew her away, back towards the waiting car.

'I think you should have a medical check-up, just in case,' said Mrs Walsh, over her shoulder, as she allowed herself to be led off.

'I bet they'd have been more sympathetic if there'd been blood,' said Kate, cheerful with relief.

'They had a point though,' said the rider. 'It was dumb. You aren't supposed to swerve for cats.'

'I'm glad you did,' said Kate.

'I'm not.' He heaved the bike away from the bole of

the tree and on to the road. Then he hitched it on to its stand and touched the scratches on the side of the fuel tank, gently, as though they might be sore. 'Look at that. This isn't mine and the owner is not going to be impressed.'

'You're American, aren't you?' said Kate.

'Canadian.' He shrugged at the bike and turned to look at them for the first time. Dark eyes in a narrow face, older than Jason, easily nineteen. He pointed behind them. 'Mill Street,' he said. 'Do you know it?'

'I live there,' said Kate. 'And Jan used to as well.'

'So can you tell me anything about the mill?'

On the far side of The Green, two car doors slammed, an engine growled irritably, and the Walshes drove away towards town.

'There's no mill,' said Kate. 'That's just a name. It's all apartment blocks and houses.'

The wind unhitched some leaves from the crooked chestnut and sent them drifting past. 'Oh,' said Kate. She looked at the tree, then revolved slowly, taking in the church with its blackened end wall, and the Memorial Garden between it and the entrance to Mill Street. 'Perhaps there was a mill once, and it was burnt down in The Fire,' she said.

He looked at her, shaking his head in exaggerated disbelief. 'Of course it was burned down!' he said. 'I know it's gone – do I ever! – but I thought there might be something left. Some ruins? An old wall maybe?'

'No,' said Kate. She was still looking around. 'I never thought!' she said. 'The Fire must have gone right over where I live – that's why our block is different – sort of newer. Jan, did you know that?'

16

'I never thought about it,' said Jan.

'And the stream?' said the rider, impatiently.

'Stream?' said Kate.

'You're really well-informed, aren't you,' he said. He could have been teasing, but if he'd been teasing he'd have smiled, and he didn't smile. 'The mill stream,' he said. 'To power the mill. I tried to find it last night but it was too dark to see properly. It has to be somewhere.'

'I saw you looking for it,' said Kate. 'From my window.' She laughed. 'I thought you were a prowler.'

He managed half a smile. 'Not a prowler, just a searcher,' he said. 'O.K., thanks anyway.' He turned and limped off, swinging his helmet, across The Green towards the shops.

'Let's follow him,' said Kate, as soon as he was out of earshot.

'Why?'

'Why not? What's he up to? What's he searching for? I think we should investigate him!'

Jan shrugged and began to move, but Kate caught her arm. 'Slow down,' she said. 'We mustn't get too close or he'll suspect.'

'I'm cold,' said Jan.

'Lighten up, will you?' said Kate, shaking Jan's arm and then flinging it away from her. 'As long as he doesn't get back on the bike we can keep him under surveillance! Come on, Jan, it's something to do!'

'He's going across to The Weaver's Arms,' said Jan. 'We can't follow him in there.'

'Weaver's Arms!' said Kate. 'Was it a weaving mill, do you think? Was the pub to do with it?'

'Who knows.'

'He's going in to ask about the mill. I bet you!'

He didn't go in, though. He glanced at the pub and then walked on by, limping a little less, towards the Witches Cauldron Gift Shop.

'That's not his kind of place,' said Kate. 'You don't often see men in there, you never see boys, and you definitely never see boys in motorcycle gear. He can't be going in there!'

He went in there.

'Come on,' said Kate. 'Run. It'll be warm inside and we can hide behind a postcard rack and see what he's up to. Hey, you realise this means it'll rain on the bonfire!'

'What are you talking about?'

'It's dry now, so he'll bring rain,' said Kate. 'Didn't you know? When a stranger rides into town he always brings change. It's traditional.'

SEVEN

The cottage that was now The Witches Cauldron Gift Shop had not been altered as much as the ones that had been converted into a newsagency and a greengrocery. Even so, it no longer looked quite the way it had when it was lived in. The modest doorway had been enlarged and the plain old door replaced with something altogether stronger and smarter. The tiny window had been extended in both directions and fitted with numerous little panes of glass, in a vague imitation of a Victorian shopfront. The small front garden had been paved over. In summer, three tiny tables stood outside, and a limited selection of tea and cakes was on offer.

The window display featured a large, white hand, with the palmistry lines marked on it in black. No one in the shop read palms, the hand was used to display birthstone rings, several on each finger. On either side of it were globe lamps, lit, each with a metal outline of a witch-and-cat-on-a-broomstick attached to the base by a thin metal upright, so that the witch and her familiar seemed to be flying past the moon. In the very front, seven black china cats, in diminishing sizes, chased each other from right to left. At the far left, in front of the smallest cat, a tiny black china frog leapt upwards on its black china stand. Witch mobiles were suspended from a rail above.

There were more witch mobiles inside, and also star and moon mobiles. They dangled on to the heads of tall customers. The rider had to put up his hand to fend them off. Gina was leaning on the glass-topped counter at the back, surrounded by silver jewellery, dishes of semi-precious stones, and crystals hanging from thongs. Her cat, which had slipped in unnoticed, settled itself on a cushion behind the counter.

Jan and Kate slid in, as silently as the cat, and stayed near the door, partly hidden by a pair of stands stocked with postcards of witches, wizards, frogs, cats, stars, moons, planets, bats, strange symbols and astrological signs.

'Hallo,' said Gina, smiling a welcome. 'Can I help you?' They both knew she wasn't talking to them. She rarely paid them any attention, and when she did it was to fix them with an expression of general disapproval. Her attitude hadn't changed since they had all been three years younger and she had been a senior prefect.

'Maybe,' said the rider. 'Was this place ever called Honeysuckle Cottage?'

'Oh – I don't know,' said Gina, thrown off balance. 'I've never heard it called that, but I suppose it might have been.'

She dipped into a box on the counter and took out a copy of a photograph of the Cauldron, taken more than a hundred years earlier, when it had been an ordinary cottage. The photograph had been reproduced many times, and small copies had their place on the postcard stand. Gina laid the picture on the counter and bent over it, as though she'd never looked at it before.

'You can see there's some kind of creeper growing all over the front,' she said, looking up through her hair and trying, unsuccessfully, to encourage him to lean over the picture with her. 'That must have been the honeysuckle.

Honeysuckle Cottage! What a lovely name!'

He pulled the photograph firmly out from under her hands and took it to a wall light to examine it closely. 'It's not very clear,' he said.

'It's very old,' said Gina. 'Taken in about 1890. The woman standing by the door was Millie Harrison.' She lowered her voice as she always did at this point, as if she was telling a secret she wouldn't have divulged to a single other person. 'It was said she was a witch,' she whispered. 'That's why the shop is called The Witches Cauldron.'

He went on looking at the picture. 'So Millie Harrison was the local witch,' he said softly.

'You can see she had cats,' said Gina. 'That's why I bring mine in every day. I think he adds to the atmosphere.' She straightened up, tossed her long hair back over her shoulders, and smiled confidingly. 'But don't worry,' she said, 'I promise you I'm not a witch!'

He didn't respond.

She tried again. 'Why are you so interested?'

'I come from here.'

'I don't think so,' said Gina, looking at him from under her eyelashes. 'I think you're from Canada.'

'I'm impressed. Most English people think I'm American.'

'Oh no,' said Gina. 'The accent's quite different.' She reached out and spun the revolving display of crystals. Rainbows danced in her hair.

Kate, behind the postcard rack, nudged Jan and mimed sticking her finger down her throat.

He carried the picture back to the counter, but he was still looking at it and not at Gina. 'We came from here originally,' he said. 'I'm in Europe for a couple of months so I decided to check this place out.'

'Are you descended from Millie Harrison?' said Gina, eagerly.

'No way!' He spoke so sharply that Gina took a small step backwards. He slapped the picture back into the box with the rest. 'My great-great grandfather owned the mill. He emigrated after The Fire. I just saw a couple of kids who said there's nothing left, not even the stream. Can that be right?'

Kate opened her mouth to speak but Jan silenced her with a glare. There was no need for Gina to know who he was talking about with such scorn.

'There's nothing left of the mill,' said Gina. 'I don't know about a stream. I've never seen one. You should go to the library, in town. They have a little local museum there – they'd be able to tell you more.'

'Is there any of the old stuff left in this cottage? Millie Harrison's stuff?' He looked urgently about him as if he expected to see her belongings still there, in the shop. 'Papers? Diaries? Can I have a look around?'

'There isn't anything,' said Gina. 'She died ever such a long time ago. Other people lived here, and then it was turned into a shop in the seventies. There's nothing upstairs but the office and stockroom. Why are you so interested in her?'

He shrugged off the question. 'She was part of my family history. Kind of. Might there be anything in the loft?'

'In the attic? Only dust. Honestly. What were you hoping to find?'

'I don't know.' He turned away. 'I'm sorry. I didn't mean to be pushy. It doesn't matter.'

'I can't show you around now,' said Gina, 'because I can't leave the shop. But if you want to come back at closing time . . .' The invitation was unspoken but obvious.

He ignored it. 'It's OK,' he said. 'No point if there's nothing there.'

Abruptly, he walked to one of the postcard racks and began to make a selection. Jan and Kate sidled away and picked through a display of witch broom key-rings, witch hat pencil sharpeners, cat-shaped erasers and cauldron candle-holders. If he recognised them he gave no sign. He snatched at the cards, dragging them out of their slots and then pushing back the ones he didn't want, his thin fingers fidgetty and tense.

Agitation seemed to be drifting out of him like an infection. Impossible not to pick it up. Gina frowned a little, and bit at the side of her nail. Kate knocked over a tiny bowl of rings and had to gather them up under Gina's angry eye. Jan found herself looking over her shoulder every few seconds.

By the time he'd chosen his cards and found the correct change he seemed calm again. But though the agitation had left him, it still existed, a faint electrical charge that drifted up and away, fading as it went, until it reached something that might almost have been waiting for it.

For now, it was feeding on any psychic energy it could find. Soon, though, it would need to start hunting, searching out someone angry, someone weak, someone easy. It was a parasite, this lost hidden thing, and like all parasites it would eventually need a host to live on . . .

EIGHT

Outside The Witches' Cauldron, eyes screwed up against the sharp wind, Jan and Kate watched as Ned went into the Weaver's Arms.

'I have *never* seen Gina put down like that!' said Kate.

'Serves her right,' said Jan. 'She thinks she's so wonderful.'

'Hey, think how our credit rating would go up if we got a date with him.'

'You're mad! We're schoolkids. We're invisible to him.'

'You don't know till we try. He's a stranger in town, he must be lonely. Maybe we could persuade him to hang out with us just for company. And then put it around that it was a date. That'd get everyone's attention! That'd get Sam's attention!'

She nudged Jan and nodded towards the next shop. Jason was outside with a customer. He had his back to them, and he was filling a brown paper bag with mushrooms from the big display table in front of the window. 'I can have Sam,' she said, 'and you can have Jason.'

'Sh, he'll *hear* you,' said Jan. 'Anyway, Sam is a Year Twelve, and Jason has a *job*. They won't look at us for ages!'

'They would if we'd dated the biker! It's OK, Jan, I do know I'm fantasising. Hey, I've just thought! The Fire didn't do *his* family much good. It burned down their mill. What's *he* going to feel about the bonfire?'

'He may not care.'

'I bet he fills his crash helmet with water and tries to put it out!'

Behind them the door to the newsagency opened and slammed, and Cal swaggered towards them, ripping the wrapper off a pack of cigarettes. As he walked right at them, Jan moved aside, but Kate held her ground. Cal chucked the wrapper in her face and walked on.

'He thinks he looks menacing,' said Kate loudly to his receding back. 'Such self delusion!' She was laughing.

'One day I'll show him!' said Jan quietly. She was tight-lipped, angry.

'And how are you going to do that?' said Kate.

'I'll think of something.'

'Jan, you've been saying that for years. Believe me, the most annoying thing you can do to him is not worry about him.'

A small white van, with ladders on the roof and A and L Builders written on the side, came down West Street and around the mini-roundabout into Green Road. It slowed as it reached the row of cottages beyond the three shops.

'Dad's home,' said Jan, watching it. 'He went up to Grandpa's yard to see if there was anything to use for firewood.'

The van pulled up in front of one of the cottages, the one that was larger than its neighbours.

'You don't move with the times, do you?' said Kate. 'It isn't your Grandpa's yard any more, it's your parents' yard.'

'Well, whatever,' said Jan. Her father got out of the van

and waved. Then he began to unclip the ladder and haul if off the roof.

'Does that mean he's going to clear out the attic now?' said Kate.

'Probably.'

'Great. Let's go and help. There might be all sorts of things up there.'

'OK,' said Jan. 'At least we'll be out of the wind.'

'What we do about the biker,' said Kate, as they headed for the cottage, 'is catch him when *he's* depressed and *we're* looking our most sophisticated, and suggest a pizza and a movie.'

'He's about as likely to date Marvin,' said Jan.

'Going out with a person is the best way to keep him under surveillance.'

'If Gina couldn't get his interest, we definitely can't.'

'OK, then,' said Kate. 'Let's find something rare and precious hidden in your attic instead.'

'It'll only be ordinary stuff,' said Jan.

'Attics are never ordinary,' said Kate.

NINE

The landlord of The Weaver's Arms carried a fresh mug of coffee across to the corner table and set it down, careful not to put it on any of the postcards strewn on the table top.

'Thanks,' said the customer, a boy in leathers with a crash helmet on the seat beside him. 'What time do you serve lunch?'

'We start at midday,' said Harry. 'You want to see a menu?'

'No thanks. I'll cruise around a bit. I might be in later.'

'Fair enough,' said Harry, and went back behind the bar.

The boy found a pen in one of his pockets and settled down to write the postcards. When he'd finished, he put the pen away and read them through while he drank his coffee.

There were three cards, each with a different picture.

The first was a black and white photograph of a creeper-covered cottage. A woman wearing a long skirt was standing at the front door. Anyone who looked really carefully could see two cats in the garden. Printed along the bottom of the card, below the picture, were the words: *The Witches Cauldron, c. 1890.*

Dear Mom and Dad, I thought you'd like a picture of her. She was called Millie Harrison. Looks pretty ordinary considering what she did. The cottage is now a commercial enterprise — note the name, above! You guessed right — there's nothing much to see here. Just like every other place I've been through in the last two days, it's building a bonfire. They still like burning things! The London cousins were friendly. Their son's my age. After this I plan to stop over with them again — then head for mainland Europe. Love Ned.

The second was a black and silver star against a purple ground. Printed along the bottom the words: ***Witch star. The pentagram, or 5-pointed star, is usually shown with one point at the top. Inverted, as here, it becomes a sign of evil.***

Dear Ben, Thought you'd appreciate a picture of an evil star! I've found my roots. Not sure why I bothered. Now I know what a depressing hole my ancestors came from. Distant cousin in London is OK. He's a courier but he's taking a week off so he lent me his Honda CX to get up here. Only come off it once so far! Staying in a hostel. Makes our Ys look like the Hilton. Yo! Ned.

The third had a bluey-green ground with, in the centre, a hologram in which little trapped rainbows fluttered. There was no printed wording.

Dear Amy, Missing you. England's a weird place. In 1605 some guy called Fawkes was caught trying to detonate gunpowder under their Houses of Parliament and every November 5th they torch an effigy of him. Forget Hitler, Mussolini, mass murderers, serial rapists — this is the one man they can never forgive. He didn't even succeed, AND they tortured and executed him at the time. Boy, can the English bear grudges! Ned, XX.

Ned finished his coffee, gathered up his cards and wandered out of the pub in search of a post box.

TEN

It was decades since the trapdoor to the attic had been opened, and it wasn't easy to release. The hinges creaked and whined with age and stiffness. Inside, the air was dead. Even when the door finally gave, and fell inwards with a thud, the dust only drifted up a little way, as though the heavy air was weighting it down.

Jan's father stood near the top of the ladder and peered into the darkness. Then he reached one hand down and Jan passed him the torch.

'Aren't you going in?' said Kate impatiently, standing beside Jan on the landing.

'In a minute.' His head and shoulders were already inside the attic and his voice was muffled, with a faint, flat echo to it. 'First I need to check where it's safe to stand.'

'We may be going to find something really valuable up there,' said Kate, contentedly.

'Doubt it,' he said, indistinctly. 'No one who lived here was ever rich.'

'There may be something that was ordinary when they had it,' said Kate, 'but it's valuable now because it's rare. The only one of its kind that's survived.' She nudged Jan. 'I can't believe you've never been up there!' she said.

'We've only lived in this house a few months,' said Jan.

'I'd have been up straight away!'

The metal ladder creaked as Jan's father climbed the

last few rungs and stepped through the attic opening. 'You can come up if you must,' he called down. 'But there's not much room and you'll get very dirty.'

The ladder rocked as Kate galloped up it. Jan followed more cautiously.

'Careful!' said her father. 'Watch your feet. Stand on the beams. Otherwise you'll go right through the bedroom ceiling.'

Climbing through the hatchway was like climbing through the skin of the house to its skeleton – right into its skull – a skull made of interlinked beams and struts, slanting upwards and meeting at the apex, like a pair of hands, wrists apart, fingertips pressed together.

The torchlight skittered around. A tiny section at a time sprang briefly into being and then vanished. Shadows leapt out of range. The dust hanging on the air smelt dry and very, very old.

Standing close together, near the opening, they watched as the torchlight searched for a way forward, but at floor level they were faced with such a confusion of crosspieces and uprights that it was impossible to see how to get further in. The attic was effectively barricaded against them to a height of about three feet.

'Does it take all this to hold up a roof?' said Kate.

'No,' said Jan's father. 'It's hard to make sense of it in this light, but most of it's stored wood. Look.' He used the torch beam as a pointer. 'These are the only ones that are part of the house.'

He began to explain the structure, how the beams supported each other, how they formed the basis of the roof, how the roof was pitched at a slant so rainwater would run off and not seep through. As he talked he controlled the torch so that the circle of light, which before had raced back and forth, now moved slowly along the timbers, from floor to ceiling. Until, abruptly, it stopped.

'Oh yuck!' said Kate.

Jan instinctively covered her head with one arm.

'Look at that!' said her father, wonderingly. 'I suppose that's what happens if you live in the dark for generations. You get distorted.'

The torch beam moved slowly on, picking out more and more of them. Spiders – but not ordinary spiders – white spiders, their bleached out bodies hanging in their tattered webs like small skeletal hands.

'What do they eat?' Kate whispered.

'Nothing,' said Jan quietly. 'They're all dead.'

'There may be live ones around somewhere,' said her father. 'I should think they'd hide from the light.'

'I'm out of here!' said Kate.

'Right, off you go. It was your idea to come up, remember.'

'So what are *you* going to do?' said Kate.

'Fetch help. I can't get this lot down on my own. I need one at the top of the ladder and one at the foot.'

'We can help,' said Kate. 'Can't we Jan?'

'We could,' said Jan, suddenly reluctant. 'Do you really want to?'

'Yes, I *do*,' said Kate. 'I get bored more quickly than you, I like a bit of action.'

'I get bored, too,' said Jan. 'I just don't mind.'

'I thought you were both terrified of the spiders,' said her father.

'We'll be all right if we don't look up,' said Kate.

'Well – we can give it a go. If you're sure.'

He wedged the torch in the angle of a rafter and then reversed partway down the ladder. 'Come on then,' he said. 'But don't try to lift anything that's too heavy for you.'

'I can't decide where to start!' said Kate. Looking down at her feet, she arranged herself carefully so she was standing in the exact centre of a beam, in no danger of stepping off it.

'We don't have to do this,' said Jan. Kate didn't seem to hear her.

The wood was stacked any-old-how. The torchlight showed a broken chair, an old broom handle, several floorboards, a lot of short chunky planks, clusters of thin, squared-off sticks, a couple of solid posts and some long narrow smooth pieces, rounded on one side and flat on the other.

'It sort of looks familiar,' said Jan.

Neither of them answered.

She wasn't entirely surprised. Her voice had sounded strange inside her own head, as though it wasn't working properly, as though its sound died away as it left her mouth. Her ears were still singing from the cold wind outside, and she was half-blinded by the battle between torchlight and darkness. She felt slightly dizzy, slightly sleepy.

'This can go on top,' Kate was saying, dragging at the chair. 'For the Guy.'

Jan heard her father's voice. He was only a few feet below, but his words seemed remote, almost unreal. 'No Guy,' he was saying. 'People died in The Fire. A Guy wouldn't be right.'

Warily, in case something scuttled out of hiding, Kate began to pull the bits of wood free and hand them through the attic opening.

Jan helped, although her arms felt strangely weak. She thought it was like trying to move under water. The stick-like pieces were easy, they could be picked up in bundles, but the planks were heavier than they looked, and several were difficult to handle because they had nails sticking out of them.

Kate, though, wasn't having any problems. She was working with rhythm and enthusiasm, and her voice never seemed to stop.

'Did you know all this was up here?' she called down through the attic opening, lowering one of the long, rounded strips of wood. 'You didn't seem surprised.'

'Jan's grandfather told me this morning,' came the voice from the landing below. 'I'd expected a bit of rubbish, but I didn't know he'd stored the whole thing up there.'

'What do you mean – the whole thing?' said Kate. 'What whole thing?'

'Don't you recognise it? It's the old staircase. Exactly the same as ours.'

'I thought it looked familiar,' said Jan, softly, to herself.

It wasn't like trying to move under water, it was like moving in a dream. Kate must be in the same dream, she thought, because there she was, dealing with the same situation. Yet she didn't seem to have the dream-weight on her limbs.

The stack decreased. The space in the attic grew. Kate moved further and further in as she worked. Jan reached out for one of the last of the planks, her hands seeming to drift through the air as she moved them towards it. She watched them close on it and pull at it. It was like looking at a stranger's hands. She thought, 'Perhaps there's not enough air up here. Perhaps I'm suffocating.'

Kate took the other end of the plank and swung it towards the opening, moving with it, leaving Jan near the back. Between them, they tipped it, so it could slide down the ladder, caught and guided from below. As Jan let go of it, she felt a thin sharp pain in one finger. She sat back on her heels and tried to see if she had a splinter, but there wasn't enough light. She put her finger in her mouth and tasted blood.

'I've hurt myself,' she said.

Kate, banging and scraping as she shifted the next piece, didn't hear her. Neither did her father, on the landing below.

She listened with growing resentment as he started to explain the history of the house to Kate. How it used to be the same size as the ones each side. How her grandfather had bought the place next door almost fifty years ago and knocked the two together. How he had spent some time deciding which staircase should stay and which should go.

'Why are you telling her?' she shouted. 'Why aren't you telling me?'

They both heard that.

Kate looked round, startled, and Jan's father called back simply, 'I thought you knew.'

The white spiders near the roof seemed to be moving gently, but whether from a draught or the peculiar effects of the torchlight Jan couldn't tell. She felt as though she'd been trapped in this forgotten place forever. She was suddenly convinced they were going to leave her up there, close the hatch, pull away the ladder and never think of her again.

She stood up, shoulders hunched against the spiders, and lifted the torch down. 'Come on,' she said, urgently, 'we've finished. I want to get out.'

She swung the torch in a great arc, and was surprised to see that she had been right, it was true, the attic was empty. There was only Kate, over on the other side, pulling at a final piece of wood.

'Shine the torch over here,' Kate said, gasping a little with the effort. 'I just want to get this last bit, but it's stuck!'

Jan sent the light in her direction, and Kate stopped what she was doing and laughed. 'Oops,' she said. 'It's part of the wall of the attic!'

Jan kept the torch beam steady. The sleepiness and dizziness had lifted, the bad dream was over and she could move normally and see clearly again. 'There was something behind that plank,' she said, edging closer along the beam. 'Mind out of the way! Let me get it.'

But Kate had seen, too, and she was already reaching into the cavity and dragging the thing out.

It was a wooden box, dull with dirt and age, about a foot square and six inches deep. Kate tugged at the lid in vain. It was locked and the key wasn't in the keyhole. 'I told you there'd be something good up here,' she said.

'Smug,' thought Jan, surprising herself. 'You sound so smug.'

Kate stood up and began balancing her way carefully along a beam towards the attic opening.

A flicker of anger went through Jan's bones. Kate always took charge, Kate was always the centre, and now Kate was taking the box away. She held out her hand. 'Give it to me,' she said sharply.

Kate stood still, at the edge of the open hatch, swaying slightly to keep her balance, looking back at her. 'I was going to hand it down to your father,' she said.

Jan put the torch on the ground so she could reach out with both hands. 'It's mine!' she said, staring Kate down, her eyes unblinking.

Kate knelt down by the hatch and held the box out over the opening. She moved slowly, watching Jan warily, almost as she might have watched an angry dog. 'How can it be?' she said, quietly. 'You've only lived here a few months.'

'Anything more coming down?' said a voice from below. 'Or are we through?'

Jan ignored it. 'My mother was born here,' she said, moving closer to Kate. 'My grandparents moved in when they were married. Before that my grandfather's parents lived here. Whatever it is, it belongs to my family. Kate, it's *mine*.'

Kate lifted the box away from the hatch opening and put it into Jan's outstretched hands.

Jan cradled it in one arm, looking down at it though she could barely see it now the torch was on the floor. She stroked it with her free hand. She could feel the soft slither of dust and the clingy sensation of shreds of cobweb. She could feel the weight, the scratches on the lid, the bruised and damaged corner.

At last she looked up. Kate was staring at her as though she wasn't sure who she was seeing.

'Jan?' said Kate. 'What's the matter? What's got into you?'

ELEVEN

The blue hatchback paused at the mini-roundabout just short of the end of The Green and then made a dog-leg, right and then left, into the narrow lane behind the cottages. Trish had planned to park in Green Road for just long enough to take in the groceries, but seeing the A & L Builders van outside the front door she gave up that idea. There were heavy parking restrictions in Green Road, and if two members of the same family blocked it at the same time there were bound to be complaints.

It was a nuisance, though. It was tricky to manoeuvre the hatchback into the garage, and once inside, it was a tight fit. Unloading was possible but very uncomfortable. She decided to park in the lane and carry everything through the garage, across the patch of back garden, and in at the back door, all the time dreading the sound of indignant horns if someone decided to leave the pub car park by the back way.

So she was already flustered when, with both hands full, she kicked the door open and saw the three figures standing around the kitchen table.

Mick didn't look too bad. He was in his working overalls and a worn-out sweatshirt and most of the new dirt was disguised by old paint and varnish stains. Jan and Kate, though, looked as if they'd used their clothes and hair as cleaning rags. They even had grimy streaks on their faces.

'What's happened?' said Trish. 'What on earth have you all been doing?'

Kate looked up and smiled. Mick, who was trying to open a large flat box on the table, grunted a greeting. Jan mumbled 'Hallo, Mum,' but didn't take her eyes off her father's hands as he tried key after key from the heap of spares in his toolbox.

Trish had brought the frozen stuff in with her and she'd got it all into the freezer by the time she understood what Kate – who was the only one taking any notice of her – was explaining to her.

When she did understand, she could hardly believe it. The hatch into the attic had remained closed throughout her childhood, her teens, her young twenties, all the years she'd lived here before leaving home to marry Mick. Her parents had never needed to go up there, and neither she nor her older sisters had been allowed to. Not that she'd ever wanted to. She'd accepted that it was off-limits and, though her parents had never said much, she'd somehow got the impression that something awful would happen if that hatch was ever opened.

It had been a childish fear – and yet, in a way, it had come true. Not three months after she'd moved back into the house, the hatch had been opened, and now the girls were filthy. They both had splinters. Jan had a nasty scratch on one finger. Kate had a jagged tear in her sleeve and seemed very subdued, either because of that or because the whole operation had tired her out. Worst of all there was a great heap of filthy old wood on the landing and partway down the stairs. Mick had put a dustsheet down, but then he must have scuffed it aside, because most of the horrible, dusty, cobwebby stuff was lying all over the carpet.

'Don't get hysterical,' he said, calmly. 'We're going to carry it all out to The Green as soon as I've got into this. See this? See what we found?'

'Even my father never went in the attic,' said Trish.

'He must have,' said Mick, in his reasonable voice, 'to put the staircase up there. It would have been before you were born, though. It's good we've got it down – it was a lot of weight for the beams to support.'

'But the mess! And look at the girls' hands! You should at least have made them wear gloves. What's Kate's father going to say when he sees the state of her! You should never have let them go up there!'

'The mess'll clean up, and I couldn't have stopped the girls. Not Kate, anyway. I'd have had to lock her out of the house, wouldn't I, Kate?'

A car horn yammered outside, and Mick detached himself from his project for long enough to help unload the hatchback. When he got back to the box he said he'd have to break it open. He hadn't been able to find the original key in the attic and none of the odd ones he'd tried had fitted.

Jan touched the lid. 'See Mum?' she said. 'See what's written on it?'

The scratches she'd felt on its surface, when she'd stroked it clean in the dark attic, formed two letters – I.L.

'I.L.,' said Trish, wonderingly. 'That must stand for Isabella Lyle. My great-grandmother.'

'That's what Dad said,' said Jan, her voice dreamy and soft. 'She'd have been my great-*great*-grandmother. What did she look like? Have we got a picture of her?'

'No,' said Trish. 'I don't think so. I've never seen one.'

Mick selected a thin blade from the toolbox. He slid it into the crack where the lid closed, right by the keyhole, and gently forced the lock. Then he put away the blade and took a step back. 'So who wants to open it?' he said.

Kate looked at Jan and Jan looked at her mother.

'Go on, Jan,' said Trish. 'You can.' She was beginning to realise she'd over-reacted – probably all to do with the fact that she was tired and the supermarket had been crowded and she hated shopping anyway. 'And then you'd better get cleaned up and let me put something on that cut.'

'It's all right,' said Jan. 'It isn't bleeding now.'

She raised the lid. It swung back on its hinges until it lay flat on the kitchen table. The box seemed to be full of dead leaves.

'Packaging?' said Mick. 'They didn't have bubble-wrap in those days.'

Carefully, Jan pushed some of the leaves aside. She was gentle with them, but they were dry and old and they crumbled as she touched them. The sound of the leaves seemed to startle the hamster and he began to scrabble urgently at the side of his cage.

'Stop it, Marvin,' said Jan, absentmindedly. 'You've had your run today.'

'Yes, there *are* things underneath,' said Trish, leaning over the box. Now she felt calmer she realised she was quite excited. A tiny piece of family history had been uncovered, after all these years.

Jan began to scoop the leaves into the box lid. A few stayed whole but most broke, or flaked into tiny powdery pieces. Kate moved as if to help, but Jan nudged her out of the way. Kate stepped back and stood still, watching her. Her frown was puzzled rather than angry. She didn't say anything.

Trish raised her eyebrows at Mick and he gave a small shrug. As far as he knew, the girls hadn't had a fight.

The box was full of paints – twelve tubes lying in a row – all with screw caps, all different colours, all partly used. Lying across the width of the box, above them, were four paintbrushes in different sizes.

'Look at that!' said Trish. 'I knew Isabella was an artist but I never imagined her paints would still be around.'

'She was an artist!' said Kate, her frown disappearing. 'Really?'

'I didn't know that,' said Jan.

'She wasn't a professional artist – she just painted for pleasure. One of her pictures is in the sitting room. Haven't you ever noticed it?'

Mick wiped his hands on his dungarees and fetched the watercolour from its place above the bookcase. He laid it on the table, beside the box.

The picture was small and a little faded, but the subject was easy to recognise. It showed a cottage, as seen from The Green, with creeper growing all over it and a small flower garden in the front.

'She didn't sign it,' said Jan.

'No, but she did paint it. Your grandfather told me.'

'It's the Witches Cauldron!' said Kate.

'That's right,' said Trish. 'It wasn't called that then, of course. This was painted when it was a proper cottage, before they messed it about.'

Jan looked up from the picture. 'What *was* it called?' she said. 'Then?'

'Oh yes!' said Kate. 'Someone was asking. Was it Honeysuckle Cottage?'

'No idea,' said Trish.

'I tell you what,' said Kate, brightening. 'You could make copies of this and Gina could sell them in the shop.'

Trish laughed and Mick said, 'Kate was determined to find something valuable in the attic.'

The feeling that had come over Jan when she first saw the box was still with her. She knew she wasn't being entirely fair, but she couldn't help it. She'd begun to resent the fact that Kate was the one with the ideas, Kate was the one who suggested things, who did things, who made things happen. She knew perfectly well that she'd always wanted Kate to lead, because everything was more fun, and easier, if she did. But that had been before.

'You could make your fortunes!' Kate was saying, joking but only half joking.

Jan looked coldly at her and said simply, 'It's not your picture. It's not up to you to decide what we do with it.'

'Jan—!' began her mother, but Kate interrupted. 'I have to go now,' she said. 'It's my turn to get lunch and I have chores to do.'

'I'm sure Jan didn't mean to snap like that,' said Trish.

'It's OK,' said Kate, over her shoulder, moving fast. 'I really do have to go.'

Within a couple of seconds the front door had closed behind her.

TWELVE

Hanging in its place on the wall, barely noticed, the small picture had been unremarkable but acceptable. Lying on the table, though, under close examination, it was a forlorn and faded thing. It wasn't even in a proper frame. The backing was thin cardboard, the glass had a couple of small flaws in it, and the black tape around the edges was coming unstuck at the corners. Even so, Jan felt a tremendous wave of affection for it. She couldn't understand why she'd never noticed it before. There was a lot of green in it – the creeper, the garden – and she touched the tube of green paint, very lightly. Her fingertip slipped briefly into the dent made by other fingers when they'd squeezed the tube all those years ago.

'Did she make pictures of rest of the village as well?' she asked.

'None that have survived, as far as I know,' said her mother. 'Did you mean to be so rude to Kate, just now?'

'She's too pushy.'

'Have you two fallen out?' said her father. 'You seemed all right with each other when you were nagging to go up in the attic.'

'We're fine,' said Jan. 'Why didn't Grandpa take this with him? It's only small. You'd think he'd want his grandmother's picture.'

'Yes, you would,' said Trish. 'I hadn't thought. Perhaps he forgot it.'

'I'm fetching him tomorrow,' said Mick, 'to see the bonfire. We can show him the paints and he can take the picture back with him, if he wants.'

'I think we should get it reframed,' said Trish. 'It's very shabby. If it comes to bits the glass'll fall out and break.'

'I could get a frame from Gina,' said Jan. 'She has lots in there.'

'That's a robber shop with inflated prices,' said Mick. 'I can make one.'

'When?' said Jan. 'This year, next year, sometime, never?'

'She's got a point,' said her mother. 'You'll keep putting it off. But I'm not sure about getting one from the Cauldron. Isn't everything covered in witches and stars?'

'No,' said Jan. 'They have ordinary frames too. Can I have some money?'

The Witches Cauldron was crowded and Gina was busy – smiling, advising, lifting things down from high shelves for closer inspection, dropping purchases into black paper bags decorated with silver stars. Each time the drawer of the till pinged open and slammed shut the draught set the mobiles drifting in circles. There was nowhere quite like the Cauldron in town, nowhere that sold such unusual gifts – or so many black cats, in china, glass, clay, candlewax and cloth.

Jan had to wait ten long minutes to hand Gina the measurements.

'Why don't you run and fetch the picture,' said Gina. 'I can't really suggest the most suitable frame unless I see it.'

'It's scenery,' said Jan. 'That's all. And the frame's rotten.'

'Do you want the same sort of thing again? What was the old one like?'

'Black sticky tape.'

'Sounds like passe-partout,' said Gina. 'No one's used that for a long time. It must be old?'

She waited, but Jan didn't offer any information. She was already unsettled by Kate's suggestion about having the watercolour copied and sold in the gift shop. Now she knew she didn't want Gina taking an interest. It was private, it was a family thing. A thought kept threading its way through her head, like the refrain from a half-forgotten song. It's mine, said the thought, it's mine, leave it alone.

'If it's a special picture,' said Gina, accepting that she wasn't going to find out any more, 'you should probably take it into Dyer's in town and have it done properly.'

'I just want to buy an ordinary frame,' said Jan. Even to her, her voice sounded harsh, aggrieved. 'That size and not expensive. You don't usually take so much interest in me.'

'You're not usually a customer. It makes me nervous when you kids hang around in here, touching things.'

'You think we're going to shop-lift?'

'Why not? People do. Here, how about this one? It's the cheapest but it's very tasteful.'

When Jan got home the kitchen table was laid for lunch so she took the picture through to the front room and sat on the carpet to take the back off the new frame in readiness. Then she started to dismantle the old one.

The black passe-partout was sticky and brittle. It peeled away in pieces, leaving little smears and grubby rolls of adhesive on the glass. Each piece clung to her fingers and she had to wipe them off, one by one, on the back of the *Radio Times*. She lifted off the cardboard and the paper that had been used as backing and put them on the floor beside her. Then she found that the painting seemed to be stuck to the glass.

By now her fingers were sticking to each other, so she ran up to the bathroom and scrubbed them clean. The sore places, where the splinters had punctured her skin, were still smarting when she got back downstairs, and the scratch was a vivid scarlet line.

She raised one corner of the picture, very carefully. What if it tore? What if all the paint was somehow lifted off and left on the glass? Slowly, slowly, slowly she peeled the paper off the glass – and it came away undamaged. Holding it gently by its edges she slid it into the new frame, face down. Then she slotted the back of the frame into place and swivelled the clips that would hold it there. She drew in an enormous sigh of air – she hadn't realised until then that she'd been holding her breath – and turned the whole thing over. It looked better than she'd expected – more cared-for – and the pale colours, without the solid black line around them, looked clearer.

She called out to the kitchen to ask what to do with the old glass. Mick came in to look at it. 'It's no good for anything,' he said, holding it up to the light. 'Scratched and flawed. I'll chuck it out. Picture looks nice. Well done.'

Jan gathered up the piece of cardboard and the piece of paper that had been used as backing. They wouldn't be any use for anything, either, and it made sense to hand them to her father to put in the bin with the glass, but somehow that didn't seem right. It seemed a better idea to open up the back of the new frame again and see if they'd fit behind the painting, where they'd always been. But before she did that, and for no particular reason she could think of, she turned them over. The cardboard was blank on the other side – but the piece of paper had a painting on it.

The painting could hardly have been more different from the soft and gentle scene she had just reframed. The colours were bright and strong, the subject violent and dramatic. A large, sombre-looking building was engulfed in red, orange and yellow flames – its tall chimney breaking up and collapsing sideways, under the impact of a jagged blue flash of lightning that stabbed out of a sky black with thick swirls of smoke.

'Look!' said Jan. 'Dad, look at this! It's The Fire! It has to be!'

THIRTEEN

A fat, hard-backed, lined notebook, red on the outside and covered with silver star and moon stickers from the Witches Cauldron. An entry for every day, sometimes two.

Saturday, November 3rd.
I made pasta for lunch. Dad never cooks pasta in the week – he knows that's what I'll do. He's asleep now. He's been on early shifts this week and it finishes him off.

This morning Jan and I helped her father clear their attic. There were some old stairs up there and we both got splinters shifting them. I think I've got all mine out.

Jan's mother was upset we'd got in such a mess. She was starting to have a go at Jan's father so I left early. He hadn't noticed the splinters. The skin on his hands is so thick they probably couldn't find a way in.

That isn't really why I left. Jan suddenly turned against me and I didn't handle it right. Maybe I hang out with her too much, but she lives so close, it's easy. Everyone else lives in town so I have to make big plans or ask for a lift or be told I'm too young to come home on the bus by myself. Also she doesn't have anyone much else to hang out with. She gets so indignant if people annoy her – she can go on about it for ages. I do like her though. I do like her, but sometimes I get fed up because I have to push her all the time to get her to do anything. But maybe I push too much. Sometimes I hear myself and I'm going on about let's do this and let's do that like some kind of manic cheerleader. I only do it to get a reaction – but I think I'd better cool it.

We found an old box of paints in the attic and I was going to hand it down to her father but she grabbed it off me as if she thought I was going to steal it or something and she looked at me as if she really hated me and I thought writing it down would make me feel better but it hasn't so I'll stop.

FOURTEEN

The whole museum was in a single spacious room which opened off the library. The library itself was in a large, oppressive, Victorian building in the centre of town. In the library, the tall bookstacks took attention away from the high ceilings and elaborate plasterwork. In the museum, though, where the metal-framed display screens stood at no more than six foot, and the wood and glass showcases were considerably lower, the sense of height and space was noticeable. The long narrow windows were set above eye level, so that although the faint grey light of the November afternoon could wash in, it was not possible to see out. This was a place where attention was supposed to be focused inwards.

It was not a modern museum. There were no dioramas, no replicas of rooms, no life-size figures in period dress engaged in occupations the living had long since abandoned. Instead, maps, pictures, newspaper cuttings and the pages of a Local History were displayed on the canvas-covered screens. Small items from the past – local finds – lay neatly labelled under glass, like flotsam left behind as a tide receded. There were stone-age hand-axes, the handle of a bronze sword, the blade of an iron dagger, a fragment of Roman mosaic, a ring with a blue stone, a Saxon brooch, a dented pewter mug, part of a leather halter, dark and cracked with age.

Kate leant on a showcase, staring in. 'There's so little,'

she said. 'What happened to all the other things people had . . .'

Jan, her back turned to Kate, was looking at a display labelled simply The Fire. Red highlighter on a map of the village, drawn in the days before the town reached out and tried to swallow it, outlined the extent of the damage. A faded photograph, taken before the disaster, showed the end wall of the mill with its great chimney, the church, and the little row of cottages that once stood between the two. Another was a close-up of the mill entrance with a group of millworkers outside, a few grinning at the camera, others clearly embarrassed. A third, strangely static and undramatic considering the subject, had been taken just after The Fire. The mill was little more than a vast mound of rubble. Two old-fashioned fire engines stood in the foreground and the small figures of firefighters could be seen, forever frozen in the act of climbing among the ruins.

The final picture, clearer, sharper, dated twenty years later, showed the new window in the west wall of the church, the clear glass set in leading which copied the pattern of the old. In one corner lay a small pile of wood – the boarding that had protected the church during the years between the destruction of the original window and the provision of the new.

Beside it, a second screen carried portrait photographs of key figures from the past of both town and village. They were mostly civic dignitaries and churchmen, but the mill-owning Merediths were there, too. She was seated, smiling, pretty. He was standing beside her, upright, unsmiling, his hand with its neat signet ring resting on her shoulder.

Jan was aware of a tingling, burning sensation in the pads of her fingers. As far as she knew, she'd got all the splinters out, but the tiny puncture marks still showed, and though the scratch hadn't been deep it looked red and angry. She hoped she hadn't picked up some kind of infection in the grimey attic. Rubbing her hands on her jeans didn't help, but when she pressed the tips of her fingers together the tingling died down.

Without turning round, she said to Kate, 'Mum says I was horrible to you. I just felt weird up in the attic, that's all.'

Behind her, Kate shrugged. 'It's OK,' she said.

'Aren't you speaking to me?'

'Yes, I'm speaking to you,' said Kate. 'I just spoke to you.'

She was slightly surprised to find herself here. Early in the afternoon she'd heard somebody tooting a horn outside, in a fancy rhythm, obviously a greeting. From the front window she'd seen the A & L Builders' van parked below, and Jan's father leaning out of the drivers' window, waving and beckoning. When she'd got downstairs and gone over to the van, he'd encouraged Jan to open an envelope she was holding on her lap and pull out the picture that was inside.

'Look at this!' he'd said. 'I'm taking it into town to show John at the museum. I thought you girls might like to come for the ride. But Kate, you must go and check with your Dad first.'

The picture of The Fire was so startling, almost like the background for a horror movie poster, that Kate had somehow let herself be swept along. Now she felt uneasy with Jan, because of the way Jan had behaved in the attic, and uneasy with Jan's father, because she could tell he was trying to repair whatever had gone wrong between them. He always wanted everyone to be on good terms with each other. It was one of the nicest things about him, but it was also one of the most annoying.

He'd talked all the way, partly to break the silence and partly because he was excited. 'For once,' he'd said cheerfully, 'the Jobbing Builder has something to show The Great Historian instead of the other way round! We went to the same school, but he was the one with the brains. I'll probably let him keep the picture for his display on The Fire – I rang Jan's grandfather, in case he wanted it, but he didn't seem interested . . .'

When they'd got there, though, he'd been disappointed. John wasn't in, just grey-haired Mrs North, sitting near the door, behind a counter stacked with Local Histories, postcards, pens and fancy notelets.

Mrs North was extremely interested in the painting, but aware that her interest wasn't enough. 'You can leave it here if you like,' she said. 'It'll be quite safe and John can see it when he comes in on Monday.'

'It's all right,' said Mick. 'No rush. I got carried away and impatient!'

'I'm not surprised,' said Mrs North. 'It's quite a find.'

'I might ask him over tomorrow evening,' said Mick, looking at the picture and talking more or less to himself. 'We can have a drink and I'll show him this and then we can go across to the bonfire.' Then he remembered he wasn't alone, looked up, smiled at Mrs North and said, 'You and your husband come too, if you like.'

Kate happened to be looking across at the pair of them as he said that, and she saw Mrs North's smile vanish. She saw her half turn away and begin tidying a perfectly tidy pile of booklets on the counter. Heard her say, quite quietly, 'No, I don't think so.'

Mick looked flustered. 'No,' he said. 'I'm sorry. I wasn't thinking. Forget I spoke.' He began to make a performance of putting the picture back into its envelope.

Kate pulled at Jan's sleeve. 'What was that all about?' she said softly.

'Don't know,' Jan whispered back. 'She seemed quite friendly with my Dad – maybe she's fallen out with Mum.'

'Maybe she owes A & L money,' said Kate.

'And Mum's written her a frosty reminder!'

'On special notepaper she stores in the freezer!' said Kate.

'And writes on with a frozen lolly!'

'A raspberry lolly,' said Kate, adding the appropriate sound effect.

Relief that the tension between them had evaporated made them both slightly hysterical.

'And now Mrs North has a frozen chip on her shoulder,' said Jan, suddenly exploding. She gave Kate a great push and Kate staggered, giggling, and then pushed her back.

They leant against each other, snorting like pigs, until they noticed that three people, over near the door, were sending puzzled glances in their direction.

The nearest two were Mrs North and Jan's father.

The third, still in the doorway, on his way in from the library, was a tall slim figure in black leathers with a crash helmet hanging from one hand.

FIFTEEN

Confronted with the stranger in the doorway, looking across at her with a faintly puzzled expression, Kate could only deal with her embarrassment in one way – she went on giggling. Jan, though, felt the smile drain away from her face, like blood from a wound. She didn't hesitate. She walked straight over to her father, took the envelope out of his hand, and marched up to the rider, sliding the picture out of its covering as she went.

'You thought we didn't know anything about the mill?' she said. 'Well we do now!' She held out the painting, balancing it on its envelope as though she was presenting it to him on a tray. 'Look!'

'Who's this?' said her father, slight anxiety sounding in his voice.

'Take care with that,' said Mrs North at the same time.

Bending down sideways to lower his helmet on to the floor by his feet, the newcomer took Jan's offering from her. He looked at it blankly for a second, and then his face showed recognition – and shock. He looked at Jan, Mrs North, Mick, and then Jan again, as if he didn't know who to address first. 'Where did this come from?' he said.

'Our house,' said Jan. 'My great-great-grandmother painted it.'

'How do you know my daughter?' said Mick.

'I'm Ned Meredith,' said the rider. 'I've been asking around . . .'

'Meredith?' Mrs North interrupted. 'Descended from the Merediths who . . .'

'. . . owned the mill, yes.' said Ned. 'I was hoping to find out more about them.'

'Well, well, well,' said Mrs North. Her tone had changed. She sounded like a teacher who has just caught someone out and plans to make the most of it. 'I never would have guessed a Meredith would have come back here.'

It was obvious Ned had heard the hostility in her voice. He hesitated, then seemed to decide to ignore it. 'Someone told me there'd be information at this museum,' he said. He looked down at the picture again. 'But I didn't expect to find anything like this.'

'How incredible!' said Mick hastily, with an anxious glance at Mrs North. 'You mean *you* have connections with the mill and *we've* just found a painting of its destruction! That's amazing!'

'Yes,' said Ned. Although Jan was closer, he passed the picture back to Mick. Jan, watching, thought how extremely different the two pairs of hands were – Ned's thin and pale with a signet ring on one finger, her father's square and reddened, with no decoration apart from callouses and one or two small faded scars.

'Must be synchronicity,' said Ned.

'Must be what?' said Kate, who had more or less recovered herself.

'It has to do with coincidences,' said Ned. 'It means if you get a lot of coincidences together there could be an underlying meaning.'

'What meaning?'

He shrugged and smiled. 'We may never find out.'

'The painting's a bit of a bonus for you,' said Mrs North, briskly. 'But we've quite a bit of other material on the Merediths here. This way.'

Her footsteps were loud and impatient on the polished wood floor.

As he followed her, obediently enough, Jan caught at Kate's arm and whispered in her ear, 'Did you notice his *hand*!'

'Not specially, why?'

'He's wearing a signet ring – I swear it's the one in the photograph.'

'I suppose it could be,' said Kate. 'It could be a family heirloom.'

'Look at him!' Jan whispered, 'He's seen it! He's noticed!'

Ned had followed Mrs North to The Fire display, and was standing staring at it while she went to the shelves at the back of the room and began to lift down bound volumes of newspapers. As they watched, he revolved the ring on his finger, then took it off and held it briefly against the photograph.

'How much of your history do you know already?' said Mrs North, thumping the volumes onto a small table.

'Some,' said Ned, replacing the ring quickly on his finger.

'Perhaps I should warn you, you may not like everything you discover.'

'How come?'

Mrs North dragged a chair up to the table and indicated that Ned should sit down. 'Your family wasn't popular around here, I'm afraid,' she said.

'Why not?' said Ned. 'They brought employment and prosperity to the area.'

Mick, visibly embarrassed, started edging towards the door, signalling to Jan and Kate that they should leave – but they were mesmerised by the scene, and he couldn't get their attention.

'They brought prosperity to *themselves*,' said Mrs North. There was a kind of triumph in her voice. It was almost as though she'd waited for this moment for a very long time. 'Safety practices cost money and slow down production. There were accidents at that mill that needn't have happened. *And* no support for those who suffered.'

'I expect everywhere was like that in those days,' said Mick walking over to join them. He'd given up trying to leave, and it seemed pointless to pretend he wasn't listening.

'No,' said Mrs North. 'Not everywhere.'

'If that's true,' said Ned, slowly, 'I guess it would explain why the locals persecuted us. I thought it was just that they resented our success – but maybe they thought they were getting their own back.'

'Nobody would have been able to persecute you Merediths,' said Mrs North. She patted the three books invitingly. 'Look in these. You'll see. You were all-powerful, locally.'

Mick reached out and put a hand on each of their shoulders, like a schoolteacher hoping to break up a fight before it can begin. 'This is all in the past,' he said. 'This has nothing to do with now.'

'They burned down the mill,' said Ned, ignoring him. 'I call that persecution.'

'No one burned down the mill,' said Mrs North. 'It was an accident. It was struck by lightning. You've seen the painting.'

Mick dropped his hands to his sides.

'I assumed the lightning flash was artistic licence.' Ned was keeping his voice very calm, very quiet, very steady.

Mrs North was quiet, too, but her eyes were hard and angry. 'The newspaper reports will confirm it,' she said, 'if you don't choose to believe me.'

'I'm sorry,' said Ned. 'But I'm afraid you haven't got the story right.'

Kate's sharp intake of breath sent a faint hiss whispering around the room, startling her as much as anyone else. Once a year Mrs North gave a talk to the school on some aspect of ancient local history. Everyone listened when she spoke and no one even considered raising a doubt about anything she said. Until that moment it had been unthinkable that anyone ever would.

'You mean you were told something different,' said Mrs North, icily. 'That's not unusual. Family history tends to get changed if it's passed on by word of mouth. People like to show their ancestors in the best light.'

'There's more to it than that,' said Ned. 'There's a diary.'

Interest fought with outrage, and interest won. 'A diary contemporary with the fire?' said Mrs North. 'The curator would like to see that. Have you brought it with you?'

'I brought it to the UK, but I left it where I'm staying. It belonged to Jane Meredith – my great-great-grandmother. The one in that photo. She writes about the fire – but she definitely doesn't mention an electric storm.'

Mrs North frowned. 'She wrote that the locals burnt down the mill?' she said. 'That's very puzzling.'

'She doesn't exactly say that. But when she writes that the mill is lost she says . . . I remember her words exactly . . . she says "I think everything has ended for us here. How can we stay in the face of such hatred." What does that sound like to you? To me it sounds like it was deliberate.'

'She may have believed that,' said Mrs North, grudgingly. 'But I'm afraid she was mistaken.'

'You're telling me the newspapers couldn't have been wrong?'

'I understood you came here to find out about your past,' said Mrs North. 'I hadn't realised you were here to deliver a lecture.'

The silence crackled with tension.

'In the diary,' said Ned, as if she hadn't spoken, 'Jane Meredith writes a lot about a woman who lived in the village, near the mill. Millie Harrison?'

Mrs North regarded him steadily. She said nothing.

'She lived in Honeysuckle Cottage – it's called The Witches Cauldron now. Someone in there said Millie Harrison was believed to be a witch.'

'Oh, grow up!' said Mrs North sharply. 'Surely you don't pay attention to that sort of rubbish!'

'Can you tell me anything about her?' Ned asked, unmoved by the outburst.

'The idea she was a witch is a puerile invention to attract customers to the shop. Just as Sunday's bonfire is supposed to bring customers to the Weaver's Arms. The landlord dumps wood out there each November, and it's always been cleared away, except this year . . .'

She raised her eyebrows at Jan's father.

'I'm sorry, Mrs North,' said Mick. 'It isn't meant to be disrespectful . . .'

'I thought these bonfires were traditional,' said Ned.

'Not here,' said Mrs North. 'That Fire was a terrible thing. It spread to the cottages so fast – the roofs fell in – everyone was trapped – most of them died. There's no photograph because when the local paper sent someone to cover the story he was so shocked by the scene he didn't even take his camera out of its case.'

'I'm truly sorry all this has been stirred up,' said Mick. 'I don't come from round here. I forget how much people were affected.'

'My grandfather was saved,' said Mrs North, ignoring him. 'He was only a baby and his mother dropped him out of a window to a neighbour. But she and his father and his sister and his brothers died in their home, burnt to death beside the Green – where some people want to hold a firework party.'

The silence in the room was a solid presence that filled it completely.

Ned broke it. 'Whatever the truth of The Fire,' he said, 'it wasn't my family's fault.'

'No,' said Mrs North, 'but they were rich and they had insurance. They could have rebuilt the mill, helped rebuild the cottages. Instead they took their money and went, leaving the mess and the grief behind them. Excuse me, I'm going through to the back room for a moment. Read the newspapers. I'll be in again shortly if you need to ask anything more.'

As the door slammed behind her, Mick said, 'Don't

take it to heart, Ned. It isn't personal. It's a difficult time of year around here.'

'I'm OK,' said Ned. 'But I wasn't ready for any of this . . . I came here thinking I'd hear the story I already know told in an English accent–with maybe a few additions. But it's kind of getting out of hand . . . See, I've read the diaries, I *know* bad things were done to my family and I know it all had to do with this Millie Harrison. Can *you* tell me anything about her?'

'No more than Gina at the Witches Cauldron will have told you,' said Mick. 'I never thought anyone took the witch idea seriously.'

'Isabella knew her,' said Jan, unexpectedly. 'She painted a picture of her cottage.'

'Isabella?' Ned looked puzzled.

'My great-great-grandmother. The one who painted The Fire.'

'Of course!' said Ned. He reached out to Jan as if he was going to catch her arm, but then dropped his hand to his side. 'She must have been here when all this was happening! Did *she* leave papers? Maybe a diary?'

'I don't know . . .,' said Jan.

'It's just possible,' said Mick. 'We found her box of paints today, in the attic. She could have left other things up there. Perhaps.'

'There wasn't anything else behind that board,' said Kate.

'There could have been!' said Jan quickly. 'I think we should look.'

'Will you?' said Ned. 'Please?'

'Not today,' said Mick firmly. 'It's too late in the afternoon and we've still got to clear away the mess we made this morning. I'm not ready to create any more just yet.'

'We don't have to make a mess,' said Jan. 'Just pulling out a loose board and looking behind it.'

Mick hesitated. 'There's a bit more to it than that,' he said.

'Like what?' said Kate, her interest caught.

'Never mind now,' said Mick. 'I'll show you. I promise. But not today.'

'Tomorrow?' said Ned. 'I'm not here for long. It would really mean a lot to me!'

'There's probably nothing there,' said Mick. 'This is the place for history. This is where you want to look.'

'I will read the newspapers,' said Ned, 'but it's obvious what they're going to say, isn't it. I'd really like to find something more personal – something written by someone who really knew . . . ' He ran both hands backwards through his hair. The leather jacket creaked and the signet ring sent out a glint of light. 'I just can't believe I've got it as wrong as all that! And I kind of need to get it right. In my head.'

'Fair enough,' said Mick. 'We'll give it a try. Come over tomorrow, after lunch. I'll give you our address.'

'He'll find it easily,' said Jan. 'He was riding round and round The Green last night – he must know it by heart.'

'I didn't know anyone saw me.'

'Oh yes. You were seen.'

'Can I come too?' said Kate.

'Course you can,' said Mick, before Jan could answer.

'A witch hunt in the morning and a bonfire in the evening,' said Kate with satisfaction. 'What a day!'

SIXTEEN

The red notebook with the star and moon stickers:

Saturday November 4th – *later. Everything's OK with me and Jan now. I think I made too much of it before. I'd planned to see if any of the others were up at the mall tomorrow. Sam sometimes hangs out there but I don't know why I bother, he always ignores me, and anyway Jan's Dad Mick plans to have another search through the attic so I'm going over there instead. I don't think there was anything else hidden with the paintbox but I could be wrong and it's exciting searching for clues in the dark. We've got a mystery now. Ned has a totally different idea of The Fire from everybody else. Mrs North gave him a really hard time and showed him all the old newspaper reports but he reckons he's got written proof of his version as well. She got really upset about The Fire. It was a bit sad.*

We might get him to come to the bonfire but we'll never get him to go out with us. I must have been mad. He's at least nineteen, even older than Sam, and we were behaving like first years when he turned up at the museum. Jan's right, he wouldn't regard us as human, let alone as dates. But what's great is Jan's interested in helping him find out more about his ancestors. I am too but Jan isn't usually interested in anything. Unless maybe she is and I only think she isn't because I'm too upfront and pushy and I don't give her a chance. I really held back in the museum, except for when we got hysterical. I think I should try to be like that more often.

SEVENTEEN

The green loose-leaf ring-binder:

Nov 4. *He turned up in the museum when we were there. His eyes are so dark . . . I feel as if he can see right into my brain. I think Dad got a fright, he thought I had a secret boyfriend. I wish! He's coming over tomorrow. Kate said there was nothing else in the attic but I said there might be. I don't know why I want him to come over, but I do. I sort of like him and I sort of don't like him. If Kate and Dad hadn't been in the museum he'd have touched my hand, I know he would. And then I'd have snatched my hand away, to show him. He thinks he's so special. I can tell he does. Mrs North was horrible to him. As if it's his fault what happened a hundred years before he was born. But I did feel bad for her. I didn't know about her family. I don't think I want a bonfire on The Green.*

EIGHTEEN

A small, cell-like room, cream-coloured walls dotted with scraps of sticky tape where posters used to hang. A narrow bed on one side, a shallow cupboard on the other, an old radiator on the wall next to it, a small table and chair under the window. A figure lying back on the bed, fully dressed, hands behind his head, staring at the ceiling. On the table, three blue airletters, all started, all open, all unfinished.

The first letter:

Dear Mom and Dad, It's starting to look like Jane Meredith got it wrong about Millie H. torching the mill. I'm staying on here a couple more days. I'll take some pictures for you. The village probably doesn't look much different now than . . .

The second letter:

Dear Amy, The hostel's in town − pretty bleak − and the heating doesn't work too well. Mostly students here. They keep telling me a rugged Canadian shouldn't feel the cold because we have serious winters. I try to explain we're used to being warm inside − in our homes, cars, shopping malls, public buildings − but I don't think they understand. Not much news. It's all kind of . . .

The third letter:

Dear Ben, I thought I was depressed yesterday but that was just a rehearsal. Half the guys in the hostel are away for the weekend and the other half have gone out drinking. I don't know why I didn't go with them. This place is doing something weird to me. Well not this place – the village. I'm becoming obsessive. I never used to be like that. I just wanted to see where it all happened, you know? But it's like going to a place and you get there and it's definitely the right place, except it's all wrong. Everything's there – the space where the mill used to be, the witch's cottage, the fire damage to the church, but it's all slanted differently. I spent two hours in the library reading local papers – I'm not kidding – and I hear myself interviewing people, asking questions that should have been asked a hundred and twenty years ago. And now I seem to have talked my way into some poor guy's loft tomorrow because there's an outside chance an ancestor who lived there around the right time could have hidden some relevant letters or diaries under the roof. This isn't me, is it? But now I've started, I can't leave it . . .

NINETEEN

Cottages which had felt the heat of the fire but hadn't caught alight, cottages with hundred-year-old smoke stains under layers of wallpaper, stood around The Green, their windows reflecting old and dusty pieces of wood, once believed to be essential parts of their structure, now rejected and stacked in a pile on the grass in the centre. It was a cold pile, not yet lit, but ready for the burning.

Maybe old wood and dust can't have feelings or memories, but something which can't *have* a memory can still *be* a memory. Collected, separated, tested, dust can be analysed, its component parts identified. And when this is done it becomes clear that there is no such thing as dust, there is only the past – minute and fragile flakes of cloth, wood, stone, leather, paper, paint, fur perhaps, bone maybe, hair and skin certainly – a record of everyone who has ever lived in a house and of everything they have ever lived with.

The cottages stood where they had stood for more than three hundred years, straining a little where doorways had been widened into arches, uncomfortable where modern windows had been forced into original walls, but enduring all the amputations and cosmetic surgery that had been visited on them. Parts which had been removed over the years but not actually taken away had been carried out to feed the growing pile – a window-frame here, a door-frame there, even an entire staircase.

And now something new was happening – an attic which had been sealed off for very many years was being opened up. The vibrations shivered through the cottages, whose attics were divided from each other by such thin boards that anyone who chose could have walked from one end of the row to the other, only pausing briefly to pull aside the flimsy barriers.

The young couple in the end cottage heard the sounds through the baby-alarm and ran upstairs to check on their son in his cot. He was asleep, and from his room they could tell it was nothing to worry about, just Mick in the large cottage next door, moving about under his own roof. No one else heard the boards being dragged away, and no one noticed the faint shudder that passed under the roofs. It only lasted a moment, shivering across the spaces above the flat over the newsagents, the unused room over the greengrocers, the stock room at the top of the Witches Cauldron, the bedrooms of the two cottages beyond.

'I'm afraid you're going to be disappointed,' said Mick. 'I think it's empty in here, but I can't see properly till I get these boards out of the way. Grab hold, will you? They may as well go on the fire.'

Ned had the torch in one hand, so Kate helped him.

'This is where Isabella's box of paints was,' said Mick. 'It wasn't hidden behind a board in *this* attic. It was lying in the next attic.'

'You don't mean I was robbing the house next door!' said Kate.

'No, you're all right,' said Mick. 'When the two houses

were knocked into one, no one bothered to link the two attics, that's all. This one's all part of our place. The hatch is probably in your bedroom ceiling, Jan, but it was blocked off and papered over years ago.'

'Did you know about this yesterday?' said Kate, accusingly.

'I always knew there was a second attic up here. When I saw you tugging at that board yesterday I think I guessed – but I wasn't sure till I came back up to try and find the key and had a closer look.'

'Why didn't you say?'

'Because you and Jan would've nagged me to break through and I couldn't be bothered.'

'I really appreciate this,' said Ned.

Jan stood slightly behind them, stooping under the angle of a beam. She was now quite certain there wasn't enough air up here, especially with four of them breathing it. She felt as though the attic was swaying, though she knew it wasn't. The moving pattern of shadows and glimmers of torchlight didn't have any meaning. It might as well have been totally dark for all she could see. She sensed Ned was near – and she knew her father and Kate were because she could hear their voices – yet she felt completely separated from all of them.

'I don't think you'd hear me even if I screamed,' she said.

No one took any notice. She wondered if she'd only thought the words, not spoken them. She opened her mouth to try again, but now Ned was talking.

'Can I go through?' he was saying. 'I'll be very careful.'

The shadows shifted again and Jan heard the sound of

someone moving away from her, towards the place where she knew the opening must be. She heard Ned's voice, urgent and excited. 'There *is* stuff here!' he said. 'Scattered all over!'

Then the choking started.

The torch fell with a clatter, and rolled, and suddenly the whole attic was rocking with light and darkness.

She heard her fathers' voice say, 'Steady,' and then he had picked up the torch and was shining it on Ned, who was doubled up, coughing, gasping, his breath hissing and whistling in his throat.

Kate reached out to thump him on the back, but he drew back his shoulder and arm and fended her off. Then he dropped on to his hands and knees and crawled towards the ladder.

'I knew there wasn't enough air,' said Jan, but her voice didn't seem to reach any of them.

She was aware that Kate had the torch, now, and her father was already on the ladder, guiding Ned down, calling for her mother, who came running up the stairs.

Once he was on the landing the choking fit seemed to pass. Ned stood still, swaying a little, his eyes streaming, breathing as if he'd run a mile. 'Asthma,' he said. 'Inhaler – in jacket – downstairs.' His voice sounded hoarse and strained.

Mick led him down, one arm round his shoulders, while Trish ran ahead calling, 'Where did he leave his jacket?'

Within a minute, the whole episode was over.

Kate knelt at the edge of the hatchway in silence for a few seconds. Then she turned to look back into the darkness.

'He doesn't have much luck here, does he?' she said. 'First he comes off his bike, then Mrs North has a go at him, and now he can't breathe.'

Jan didn't respond.

'Might as well see what he found,' Kate said, her voice subdued. 'Shall we? Do you want to?'

Jan stood where she was, holding on to a beam, breathing in and out carefully, testing that she could. She almost thought she still heard the choking sounds, as if they had travelled the full length of the row and were now echoing softly back again.

'Shall I go and see, then?' said Kate, at last. 'If I find anything I'll bring it out so you can look at it first. OK?'

Jan didn't answer. All she wanted was to get out and go downstairs, but she was afraid to move when she couldn't see where to tread safely, and Kate had taken the torch into the second attic.

Jan heard her moving slowly around, heard her say, 'There isn't anything in here – what did he think he saw?' Then, 'Oh yes! All scattered, like he said!'

Impossible to judge, by the stealthy sounds, whereabouts Kate was or what she was doing until, eventually, she was back, shining the torch on something in her other hand. It looked like pieces of greyish-white cardboard, or like an art-pad that was falling apart as Kate held it.

'We'd better go down,' said Kate, 'and see if he's all right.' She shone the torch near Jan, trying to see her without dazzling her. 'He *will* be all right, won't he?' she said. 'He did look awful. And he sounded worse. Oh Jan – you don't think he could die, do you?'

'Possibly he will,' said a voice out of the darkness. 'And

possibly he's the last male of the line and that'll be an end to them.'

'*Jan!*' said Kate. 'That's a horrible thing to say!'

Panic gave Jan her voice back. 'That wasn't me talking!' she said. 'Kate, that wasn't me.'

'It was you!' said Kate. The torch beam was no longer steady. 'Jan, it was your voice. And I saw your mouth moving!'

TWENTY

The paintings were in surprisingly good condition, considering they seemed to have been thrown into the attic and left there for several decades. Each was protected by a sheet of tissue paper, lightly held at all four corners with a tiny piece of the same black passe-partout that had been used to frame the portrait of the cottage that was now the Witches Cauldron. The tissue had kept them more or less clean, and there had been no light to fade the colours.

It was a subdued group that stood around the table to look at them.

Jan and Kate had brought them downstairs and into the front room, rather self-consciously carrying half each. They had come to a silent agreement not to talk about the words Kate knew she had seen Jan speak, the words Jan knew she had not spoken.

Ned was over the worst, now, but his face was still pale and his voice harsh and shaky. 'I'm usually OK,' he said. 'I stirred up some dust. Suddenly it was all in my face and I breathed it in.'

Trish, helping to peel off the shreds of passe partout, kept looking over her shoulder at the stairs.

It was twice, now, that the attic had been entered – and the hatch had been left open for two days and a night. It was silly, she was sure, to let it bother her – just because her parents hadn't wanted their children to play up there, among dust and splinters. She couldn't help it, though – couldn't get rid of the feeling that an important taboo had been broken, a dangerous line crossed.

'Mick, are you going to close up that attic again?' she said. 'Now it's all cleared out?'

'Sure,' said Mick, also picking away at the black sticky tape, working carefully and delicately despite his large fingers.

'Well will you do it soon?' said Trish. 'It makes the house feel insecure. Like leaving the back door open or something.'

'Was there anything else up there?' said Ned, without much hope.

'No,' said Kate. 'I did look carefully. Really. Just these.'

'I wonder why they framed one of her paintings and hung it on the wall and then chucked all the rest up there,' said Mick, standing back a little to look at the four pictures, now uncovered on the table.

'They're not exactly high art,' said Ned, cautiously.

'She came from a very ordinary working family,' said Trish. 'People like her didn't usually draw or paint, not in those days. I think she did very well.'

Jan reached out and arranged the four pictures in a square, two above and two below, as they might have been displayed on a wall.

'That's my point,' said Mick. 'These are no better or worse than the one that was put on show. Why weren't they all framed?'

The picture that lay top left was the simplest – a blue-green field with a fence running partway across it and blurry trees rising out of a ground mist behind it. There was very little detail.

Next to it was another field, this one full of sheep, with a fence all the way around it.

Bottom left was a fairly detailed study of a farm cart, stacked with milk churns.

Next to that was something more dramatic. It wasn't very skillfully executed, but it was very easy to understand. It showed a side view of a horse, its forelegs braced, its head and neck dipping down, its rider in the act of falling off forwards, over the horse's head. It was obvious the horse had stopped suddenly. A few dark brush strokes in the long pale grass in front of it hinted at the likely cause. Something had startled it – a small animal of some sort, possibly a cat.

Ned drew in his breath sharply, pulled out one of the upright chairs and sat on it.

'Are you all right?' said Trish. 'Is it the asthma again?'

Ned shook his head.

'She did like disasters, didn't she?' said Mick.

'You mean The Fire and the man falling off his horse?' said Kate.

'I mean all of them,' said Mick.

'The others are just local scenes,' said Trish.

'Look closer. Look at the cart carrying the milk churns.'

It was subtly done and easy to miss. The rear offside wheel of the cart had broken clean in half. The two halves still formed a circle, but it was not a perfect circle. There were tiny gaps in the rim, top and bottom, and one half of the wheel was at a very slight angle. Half the wheel had just begun to fall away – in the very next second, the whole cart would crash onto its side, throwing the churns into a ditch.

'That's brilliant!' said Kate. 'Painting an accident just before it happens! That's really slick!'

'And look at the field,' said Mick. 'It's flooded. That's water, not grass – see how she paints grass in the others. She makes tiny little lines.'

'I see what you mean,' said Trish. 'But it doesn't have to be a flood, it could be a pond.'

'No, that fence doesn't just stop. Look. It gets shorter and shorter and then in the middle, where the field dips, it disappears underwater. It's definitely a flood.'

'So what's wrong with the sheep?' said Kate.

'They're kneeling, aren't they. That's not right.'

'Aren't they just resting,' said Kate.

'No. They're kneeling with their front legs, their back legs are upright. That's a sign of foot-rot.'

'Oh, yuck!' said Kate.

Mick went over to the bookcase and lifted down the small, reframed painting that hung above it. He put it on the table beside the others. Ned was the only one who didn't lean forward to look. Their breath misted the glass. But nothing bad seemed to have happened to the cottage, and nothing bad seemed about to happen, either.

'Well now we know why they kept this one on show,' said Mick, returning it to its hook. 'It's just a nice little picture.'

'These have all got numbers on the back,' said Trish, turning them over. 'Very faint, in pencil.'

'Dates?'

'Oh yes, they could be. And then other numbers as well, below the dates. I wonder what made her choose these subjects . . .'

'Probably all local events,' said Mick. 'I wonder if she

thought she could sell them to the local paper, make a bit of extra dosh.'

'The accident with the horse was definitely a local event,' said Ned, quietly. 'In Jane Meredith's diary – she writes about it. It happened to her son. He was out riding and his horse threw him.'

'Was he all right?' said Kate,

'No. He was horribly injured. He died three days later. He was her eldest son – if it had happened to her second son I wouldn't exist.'

'Oh, Ned!' said Trish. 'So it must have been quite a shock, seeing this.'

'It was,' said Ned. 'I don't know why – it's not as if I ever knew him.'

'But he was your relative,' said Jan.

'Yeah, but generations back,' said Ned. 'I think what gave me the shock was that it's kind of like seeing the diary illustrated. My great-great grandmother was writing about bad things that happened, and at the same time your great-great-grandmother was painting them. It just made me feel – weird – for a moment.'

TWENTY–ONE

The bonfire on The Green, such a cold, dark thing at this stage, had grown in less than two days into a construction almost as high as the town bonfire, which people had been working on for months. The old broken-up staircase, carefully stacked, had increased it to such a size that people who hadn't given it much thought before were encouraged to add to it and, even this late in the day, more were arriving with their contributions.

Sometimes a piece of wood, ill-balanced, would fall off and strike someone, but there were no real injuries, and mostly it was built well, as if everyone had waited such a long time for the chance they were determined to do it properly.

The base was so wide that eight people joining hands would barely encircle it, and the height was already over six feet. The church, the chestnut tree, the old cottages had not witnessed its like for over a hundred years – though before that, the November fires had been a familiar sight locally.

It was unstoppable now, its sheer size and density seeming to demand a crowning touch – a sacrifice. Yet it was to be denied the traditional substitute, the guy with its raggy face gaping in the flames . . .

In the misty, grey, dying light a dozen or more figures moved around the growing mound, its servants, feeding their creation. They could have come from this century, the one before, or further back still. Their breath on the air was like smoke.

Harry, the landlord of The Weaver's Arms, had called in all his staff and was instructing them in the preparation of suitable food. He'd planned a small ceremony for the lighting – timed for seven o'clock – and a modest display of fireworks to be set off shortly afterwards. All was going well, although twice a door had slammed unexpectedly, and the second time the vibration had knocked a glass off the bar with a shattering crash.

Kate's father, Jim, was outside already, placing buckets loaned by the pub at strategic intervals, some filled with water, others with sand. He was glad to help. His family had been firefighters for generations, his great-grandfather's image forever locked in a photograph in the museum, in the act of sifting through the charred ruins of the mill. Jim, though, had been lame in one leg since birth and wasn't considered suitable. He liked his job, setting advertising copy for a consortium of local papers, but it wasn't what he would have chosen.

The inhabitants of the executive houses in Mill Street, newcomers all, were planning to go outside as soon as it was dark.

In the Mill Street flats, choices were being made – the fire on The Green or the fire in Central Gardens in town. The one was closer and more convenient, the other was traditional, municipal, and certain to have a bigger fireworks display.

There was also a third choice, one that was being made in some of the flats, a few of the cottages, and one or two houses deeper in the village, away from The Green – a studious boycott of the whole thing, with curtains tightly closed.

In the cottages beside The Green, most people had decided to go out and enjoy what was on offer when the time came. Some had even invited visitors to join them. Only the Walshes, and the young couple with the baby at the far end, preferred to enjoy the spectacle from their front windows, where they wouldn't have to suffer the cold, the damp, or the smell of charred timber and gunpowder.

The newsagency was open – there could well be a market for chocolate bars – and though the greengrocers was closed, Jason was outside with a borrowed brazier, making ready to roast chestnuts.

Gina didn't intend to open up The Witches Cauldron. She didn't want children with sparklers in among the cards and candles. But she had agreed to drive in nearer the time and help out at the bar in The Weaver's Arms, if she was needed.

Harry was expecting to be very busy. Despite the fact that it was such a last minute enterprise, word was out. Mostly it had been carried back to town by people who had gift-shopped at the Cauldron on Saturday. Now, on Sunday, Harry had already taken thirty phone calls from people checking the story was the truth and not a rumour. The Central Gardens affair might be bigger and grander, but the party on The Green had curiosity value. Also, as some people had been telling each other all day, it would have far more atmosphere, being held in a real village on a genuine village green. A sense of anticipation and mild excitement was building.

Throughout the fabric of the cottages, though, there

was a tension that had very little to do with their inhabitants.

It was fully awake now, whatever it was, and feeding on any available energy – and there was plenty of energy around. It could do so much already, after all the barren years, but it wanted more. It wanted, as it had always wanted, to have physical impact – to change, reshape, destroy. And that meant using things which had physical substance. It wasn't in a hurry. It was experimenting. It was trying out dust and small animals, doors and glass tankards, broken wood and living human bodies. It was pulsing with its own rhythm: now dispersing through the attics, under the floors, behind the walls; now gathering itself together in a knot, like a blister, that made the buildings themselves uncomfortable.

It fed on the energy of everyone who came within its sphere, but this was not solely a one-way thing. Some of the energy flowed back to its various sources again, lightly contaminated with a mixture of emotions – apprehension, anger, bitterness – and fear.

TWENTY-TWO

All but one of the people in the large double-cottage could give a reason for the agitation or excitement he or she felt, but not one of them knew where it really came from. Not yet.

Ned believed it was the shock of finding bits of his family's past and discovering they didn't fit in with the story he'd always been told.

Trish thought it was the disturbing awareness of the gaping attic, which Mick had not got around to closing off and sealing.

Grandpa Lyle put it down to the unsettling emotions of being brought back to his own house and knowing he didn't belong here anymore.

To Kate it seemed it was her anxiety about Jan, and about whether she ought to mention Jan's odd behaviour to anyone.

John, delighted by his old school friend's offer of a contemporary painting of The Fire for his museum, was certain it was the unexpected pleasure of this wealth of local history, including the promise of a chance to read an old hand-written diary.

Mick was convinced it was everyone else's tensions, affecting him. He liked everyone around him to be calm and at ease with each other, and this afternoon they clearly weren't.

Only Jan wasn't sure. She could have blamed it on the

unaccountable rage she felt when anyone handled the old wooden box of paints – but then what could she blame for the rage itself?

The small front room felt very crowded. Grandpa Lyle was a big man, bulky and broad-shouldered, and he sat in the centre of the small sofa, his hands resting on the seat cushions each side of him, leaving no room for anyone else. Mick sat in the armchair on one side of him, and Trish in the chair on the other – though she kept jumping up, first to put the kettle on, then to check if it was boiling, finally to make tea.

Ned and John seemed to have taken over the table. They were sitting on straight-backed chairs on each side of it with the box and the pictures between them and Ned's precious diary, revealed at last, lying in front of him, under his hands.

Kate was hovering by the window, half listening to the talk in the room but mainly watching the build-up of activity outside.

Jan didn't know where she wanted to be. In the end she chose the upright chair just inside the front door – the one where letters to be posted were usually left. Something rustled as she sat down and she pulled the local paper out from under her and dumped it on the floor. 'No To Green Fire' said the headline at the foot of the front page.

John – slow, quiet John – examined each painting carefully and then turned his unhurried attention to the box of paints. Ned, opposite him, his fingers tapping softly on the old blue book under his hands, hardly glanced at what was on the table, instead he stared at John, desperate for his attention, desperate for information. John was perfectly unaware of this and Jan, watching, found herself thinking, 'Good, let him wait.' Then she wondered why she'd thought that. She was half afraid it might have something to do with Ned's dark good looks and the fact that he was taking no notice of her at all. But no, she also felt irritated with John, handling Isabella's property as if he had a right, and John looked older than her father – even though he wasn't – and was definitely not good looking.

'This is very nice,' said John. 'Paint in the original lead tubes. You wouldn't get those now.'

'Put it in your museum,' said Grandpa Lyle. 'If you like it so much.'

'Do you mean that?'

'Take the pictures, too, if you want. They're not very nice subjects.'

'Is that why they were hidden away under the roof?' said Mick.

'My father did that. You'd have to ask him. If he was still here. I never remember Grandma doing any painting.'

'But you had one of her pictures on the wall,' said Mick, pointing to it.

'She did paint once. But she'd long given up by the time I was born.'

'Why did you put the stairs in the attic?'

'Not in *that* attic, I didn't,' said Grandpa Lyle. 'That attic was never opened in my lifetime. I put 'em in the attic above there,' he pointed across towards the barely used dining room, on the other side of the front door, 'above that half of the house, the new half. Thought the wood might come in handy.'

'But it didn't?'

'Just never got around to going up there again.'

'I think our family has a bit of a phobia about attics,' said Trish. 'Now I look back I don't remember any of us even *wanting* to play up there!'

'Where's Marvin?' said Grandpa. 'I want to play with Marvin.'

Jan fetched Marvin from his cage in the kitchen, went up behind the sofa and put him on her grandfather's shoulder. He reached up and lifted the hamster gently down and then sat pouring him from hand to hand, as if he was sifting grain.

The peaceful scene was too much for Ned and he exploded with, 'Please! *Please* will somebody give me some information. I *know* The Fire wasn't the simple accident everyone around here thinks. I *know* something happened. Will you listen to this?' He opened the old blue book somewhere near the middle. Jan, on her way back to her chosen place on the chair near the door, saw that he had marked the place with a length of cotton. He read, '*Twenty-first of March, 1880. I think everything has ended for us here. How can we stay in the face of such hatred? We saw the smoke and the glow from the house, and I knew what she'd done. The fire engines were there before us but there was little they could do. The wind blew the flames on to the cottages of Church Row and the thatch caught and all efforts were naturally diverted to try and save them. It was terrible to see. They were all lost and some of the cottagers with them. I cannot believe such a cruel end was intended for those innocent folk. Had the mill stream not been such a good source for the pumps, I think the church might have been lost, also, and the houses on the other side of the green. The Chief Fire Officer has told us that never, in all his experience, has he encountered such a conflagration. I cannot stop thinking of what I was shown. It seems impossible, yet it is true.'*

He flung himself back in his chair. There was a tiny pause, then John said, 'I understand why you thought the fire was started deliberately. She does make it sound like that. It must have been really strange for you, coming here and finding everybody had a different perception of events. And nothing tangible left to see.'

'Not even the stream,' said Ned, flatly.

'I can tell you,' said John, 'that the mill wasn't using water-power at the time of the accident. They'd gone on to steam. In fact, there are minutes of a directors' meeting which show the Merediths were considering electrical power. But the stream was still flowing, which was useful for the firefighters. Then about thirty years ago a dam and reservoir was built out in the hills behind the town and our stream is one of three that feed it. It hasn't flowed as far as this since then.'

'*Thank* you,' said Ned, with some sarcasm. 'Almost my first piece of information. *Now* can you tell me about Millie Harrison and Honeysuckle Cottage.'

John smiled. 'I had a look at the census of 1881 earlier today,' he said. 'People *are* looking out for your interests, however it may seem to you. Both Mrs North and Mick have been on to me about your Need to Know. But according to the census the cottages around The Green were known by numbers only. The name must have been informal – descriptive.'

'I do appreciate your help,' said Ned. 'It's just . . .'

'. . . that I seem rather slow?' said John.

'I remember Millie Harrison,' said Grandpa Lyle, unexpectedly, apparently talking to the hamster cradled in his hands. 'Don't remember much. I was about ten when she died. Us children were scared of her. We kept out of her way.'

'Was she friendly with your grandmother?' said Mick. 'Isabella?'

'If she was, they must have fallen out. They weren't friends when I was a child.'

'But the picture . . .' said Mick.

'It was a pretty cottage,' said Grandpa. 'Still is, in spite of the mucking about it's had. You don't have to be friends with a person to think their cottage is pretty.'

'According to the diary she was really bad news – scary – malicious,' said Ned. 'Is that how other people saw her? Do you remember?'

'Us children called her a witch.'

'You know what children are like . . .' Mick began.

'My great-grandmother thought the same thing,' said Ned. 'Listen to this entry – *I can hardly believe I am writing this, but I half-believe she is a witch. No one who offends her seems to go unpunished. It appears she had hopes of Mr Rogers for her daughter. A foolish conceit since his family is far superior to hers. Yet no sooner did he marry Miss Williams than his fields flooded, his sheep sickened, and within months he was bankrupt and forced to leave his land.*'

'It's worth remembering,' said John, 'that there were disastrously wet seasons in the late 1870s. Flooding and sheep rot weren't at all rare, nor was it rare for a farmer to go bankrupt around that time. Quite common in fact.'

Ned shrugged. 'Whoever named The Witches Cauldron must have thought there was *something* in it,' he said. 'Mrs North said it was a commercial gimmick, but I'm certain it was more than that.'

'Ah,' said John. 'You see, Mrs North is related to Millie Harrison. Mrs North's grandmother was Millie Harrison's niece. Naturally she's a bit defensive about the witch rumours.'

'Oh, right!' said Ned. 'No wonder she hates me! It must be in the blood. I wish I'd known that when I talked with her – no wonder she wasn't too thrilled when I said one of her ancestors could be a witch.'

'It was all such a long time ago,' said Mick, wistfully. 'It might be time to forget all that.'

'I think Millie Harrison's brother died in an accident at the mill,' said Grandpa Lyle. 'Does someone want to take this animal away now? It's getting tired.'

Jan took Marvin from her grandfather. She felt obscurely threatened, but she didn't know why. No one in this room would wish her any harm. She held Marvin against her face and his soft warmth calmed her.

'Funny name, the brother had,' said her grandfather. 'I can't recall it.'

'Elias,' said John. 'Millie Harrison's brother Elias worked at the mill, and yes, he died in an accident. She certainly had cause to feel bitter. Oh, one other thing I discovered in the census. In 1881 Millie Harrison was living with the Merediths.'

'No!' said Ned, obviously startled. 'That can't be right!'

'Oh yes, that rings a bell,' said Grandpa, at the same time. 'She used to be 'in service' with them. A maid of some kind, I suppose. That would have been long before I was born, she was old when I remember her, but people still talked about her. It stuck in my mind because I didn't know what 'in service' meant. I thought it had something to do with the army.'

'But that doesn't make any sense!' said Ned. 'Jane Meredith was afraid of her. Have her in the house! Breathing the same air! Near her children! Never! Jane would never have allowed that!'

John cleared his throat, almost apologetically. 'It's very unlikely the census is wrong,' he said.

Grandpa Lyle made a sudden movement as if he was about to get up. Then he sank back with an exasperated sigh and said, 'Why can't anybody ever leave things alone!' It didn't sound like a question.

'Dad?' said Trish.

'Digging out all this rubbish.' Suddenly the veins were standing out on his forehead. 'Going into the attic . . .'

'You said it was all right!' said Mick, visibly shaken.

'Not much point saying no after you'd done it, was there.'

'You told me there was stuff in the attic that could go on the fire,' said Mick, patiently. 'That's why I went up there. I wouldn't have gone up if you hadn't said that.'

'I said *that* attic, above *there*,' said Grandpa. He had subsided a bit and he was beginning to mumble, as if he wished he hadn't started on the subject. 'I meant you to take the staircase. I couldn't know you were going to break into the *other* attic, could I?'

'I'm really sorry,' said Mick. 'I didn't think you'd mind.'

'I *don't* mind. Why should I? It isn't my house now, it's yours. Nothing to do with me.'

'You didn't say anything when I told you what we'd found,' said Mick.

'What did you expect me to say?'

'Dad,' said Trish, 'Is it that you're upset about the

bonfire? You should have said if you'd rather not be here tonight.'

'Oh?' said Grandpa. 'Should I have said no thank you, I'd rather sit alone in my one room listening to the man next door coughing and the woman upstairs creaking about and dropping things?'

Mick got to his feet. 'Where's my coat?' he said. 'We're supposed to be enjoying ourselves. Let's go out there and join in.'

'Oh yes!' said Kate, turning away from the window. 'It's almost dark and there are so many people out there already . . .'

'Yes, let's go and watch fireworks,' said Grandpa Lyle, heaving himself upright. 'It was all a nasty business, best forgotten.'

'Oh I don't know,' said Trish, 'I don't know if it *can* be forgotten. Everyone's all worked up now. And our family suffered too, don't forget – when the mill was lost, and the jobs went . . .'

'It's quite a clear-cut division,' said John mildly. 'Those whose families lived here at the time are against it – newcomers are in favour. Very understandable. Loyalty to ancestors.'

'Or a memory stored in the bones,' said Grandpa Lyle, but so quietly that only Jan heard him.

'Oh Ned!' said Trish. '*Your* family! No one's asked you how *you* feel about it.'

'Come on,' said Mick, unusually impatient, hunching himself into his coat, 'We're not lighting *The* Fire – we're not burning an effigy of the mill!'

'I'm OK,' said Ned. 'I don't go in for all this grudge stuff. It's Guy Fawkes I feel sorry for. 'Rest in peace' seems a little overdue, in his case.'

'The bonfires aren't really about Guy Fawkes,' said John. 'The idea of burning the guy has locked on to a much older tradition.' He nodded towards the local paper, where it lay on the floor. 'My article this week is all about the fires, if you're interested. The Night of Fires and the Dead!'

TWENTY-THREE

Friday's local paper, glanced through without much attention by Trish and then Mick, left on the chair by the front door, sat on, dropped on the floor, now folded crookedly and a little creased.

The article was on an inside page, under the heading 'Night Of Fires And The Dead', and beside a photograph of a rocket exploding into a great circle of stars in the sky. The caption under the photograph read: *Last year's firework display in Central Gardens*.

'Night Of Fires And The Dead.

by John Leigh

This is the time of year for the early winter ceremonial fires. Tuesday 31st is All Hallows Eve, or Halloween, and Sunday (remember, remember!) is the 5th of November. It is no accident that these two festivals are only four days apart in our calendar. Their relationship is, in truth, very close – so close that it can be argued they are two parts of the same thing.

The effigy on top of the bonfire may commemorate the man who led the conspiracy to blow up King James I and both Houses of Parliament in 1605, but the fire underneath him has a symbolism that is far older. In it are echoes of the ancient Celtic festival of Samain, which also resonates in the celebrations of Halloween. The Samain fires were lit to revitalise the dying sun. They were fires of renewal, cleansing fires, designed to burn all that was evil and to strengthen all that was good.

Ritual fires are significant in many cultures – and so is the belief that, at this time, the dead are permitted to return briefly, and spend a few hours among the living they have left behind. Whether the dead are welcomed or feared depends on the beliefs of the living. Are these benevolent dead, back among us to reassure us of their continued existence in some form or other, perhaps even to help us in some way? Or are they malevolent dead, here to wreak havoc and vengeance?'

Either way, when you set a match to the candle in your pumpkin lantern, or light the bonfire you have been building for weeks, you can be sure that your actions would seem very familiar to the ghosts of your most distant ancestors.

[The bonfire in Central Gardens will be lit at 7.30, fireworks at 8pm].

TWENTY-FOUR

John made the discovery about the pictures not two minutes after Trish and Mick had gone on ahead with Grandpa Lyle to The Weaver's Arms. Ned was putting a film in his camera, ready for the bonfire. Jan had just shut Marvin in his cage and was pulling on her jacket. Kate was waiting impatiently by the door.

John was still at the table. He'd turned the pictures over on their faces and was examining the numbers on their backs. 'I've hit on a bit of a puzzle,' he said. 'The date on this one,' he pointed to the picture of The Fire, whose strong colours showed faintly through the paper, '– is wrong.'

Ned clicked the back of the camera case closed and looked up with a frown. 'Maybe it isn't meant to be the date of The Fire,' he said. 'Maybe it's the date she painted the picture.'

'No,' said John, 'She's dated it two days *before* The Fire.'

Kate was close enough to Jan to feel a sort of shiver run through her. 'Are you all right?' she said.

'I'm OK – I just felt – no, it's gone now.'

Ned put the camera on the table and sat down again. 'You wouldn't think she'd get that wrong,' he said.

'No, you wouldn't,' said John. 'Some dates perhaps. But *that* one . . .'

Ned pushed the camera aside and picked up the diary

again. 'What's the date on the picture of the man falling off the horse?'

'February 10th,' said John, leaning across to peer at it.

Ned searched for a page – found it – read aloud slowly. '*February 11th*!' he said, '*Today it happened. Graham's horse fell and threw him. Edward was forced to shoot the poor beast.*' He looked up from the book. 'Graham was the Meredith's eldest son.' He read on, '*February 13th – Graham's injuries were more severe than we at first realised. Surely things will not go as far as I now fear.*'

In the silent room the thin old paper seemed to whisper as Ned turned two more pages. 'And here's the shortest entry in the diary – February 14th – she writes *My son is dead.*' He closed the book.

Outside, a firework squealed into the sky. Kate looked through the window in time to see it spit out two stars and drop to earth, a tiny red dot.

'Was that the display starting?' said Kate. 'Oh no, it came from one of the back gardens . . .'

No one took any notice of her.

Jan realised she had almost stopped breathing. She drew in air in a gasp, like a long sigh. She didn't want to go outside, but nor did she want to stay in and hear the diary and the pictures analysed. She was aware of Kate fidgeting, anxious to get on to The Green among all the people, but not wanting to leave her behind. She was aware of John and Ned, facing each other across the table in earnest discussion. But it was as though she couldn't focus on any of them. They were two-dimensional patches of colour, Ned all in black, John in shades of grey, Kate green and purple. She knew she was in the room with them but somehow she didn't know whereabouts in the room she was. It was as though she was drifting through it, like a wraith, yet she knew she couldn't be because no one was looking at her strangely.

She heard Ned say, 'Either Isabella got her dates scrambled or else she painted both the events before they happened.'

She heard John say, 'I don't think the second idea is a real possibility. Do you?'

Then Ned tipped his chair back from the table, balancing it on its back legs. 'I'll tell you what *I* think,' he said. 'I think Millie had second sight.'

John raised his eyebrows.

'I think the ideas for all these pictures came from her. I think Millie told Isabella what to paint – and I think Millie showed the painting of The Fire to Jane *before it happened*.'

John opened his mouth to speak, possibly to object, but Ned talked on – 'It would explain something Jane says – when she's writing about the fire – she says she was shown something, and I think she was shown *this* picture.'

He was turning the pages of the diary so urgently now that it seemed likely he would tear them. John reached out a restraining hand, but Ned had found what he was looking for. 'Listen! *Today she came to me with her view of the future. It frightened me, as she intended.* I thought it meant Millie *told* her about the future – but now I think she showed her a picture – "her view" – It was a picture, a painting. Millie had second sight! It's the only explanation. It reconciles the different versions perfectly.'

Jan, drifting, listening, heard another voice, which after a moment she realised was her own, asking why everybody was talking about Millie, why it couldn't have been Isabella, the painter herself, who had the second sight.

If Ned heard her, he chose to ignore her. 'Millie probably saw pictures in her head,' he went on, 'and rather than just *tell* people what she'd seen, she got her friend and neighbour Isabella to paint her predictions. And when she showed the pictures, people assumed she was threatening them. Maybe she never meant to threaten – maybe she only meant to warn. But when the things she'd warned about actually *happened*, people decided she had to be a witch!'

Outside on The Green the light had died away, and the street lamps had taken over. Inside the room the darkness had built up so slowly they had barely noticed that they were seeing by the artificial light through the window. The five paintings, face down on the table, glowed white in the gloom. The headlamps of cars, arriving for the display, sent yellow searchlights chasing across walls and ceiling.

'I can't see a thing!' said Kate suddenly, and switched on the centre light, startling everyone, including herself.

The change was dazzling. John took his glasses off and rubbed his eyes.

'The part I don't understand,' said Ned, 'is why Millie didn't predict her brother's death. Unless there's a picture missing.'

'That knocks your theory a bit,' said John. 'She doesn't appear to have foreseen any of the mill accidents, and there were several, though only two deaths. Her brother Elias died instantly – the other fatal injury was originally quite minor, but it turned gangrenous.'

Jan was aware that he looked at her at that point, as if to include her in the conversation, but she turned away, ignoring him. She began to move slowly around the room, putting on the side lights – one on the shelf in the corner by the kitchen door, one on the end of the mantelpiece, one on the table near the stairs. She wanted to turn out the centre light, she couldn't bear its brilliance. Also she needed to do something to reassure herself she really was physically present, that she really did occupy a particular space in the room, that she really could choose to walk from one part of it to another and carry out simple actions.

She heard the others talking, but it was like hearing voices on radio or television. It didn't seem necessary, or even possible, to respond.

A peppering of short, sharp explosions rattled into the air, following by series of heavy bangs, two seconds apart, which sent brief blazes of white light into the room. Kate at the window reported Cal and his two henchmen on the grass opposite. 'They're going now,' she said. 'They've run out of bangers.'

The sounds acted like a starting gun on John, who set off for the pub, conscious that staying away any longer might seem impolite, as if he was more interested in late-nineteenth-century documents than his friends.

'I'll come back here afterwards,' he said to Ned, as he left, 'And perhaps we could meet at the museum tomorrow, as well? We have a lot to talk about. This is all most intriguing.'

Ned nodded, but he stayed where he was, at the table. As the door closed behind John, he gave a little shake of his head, as if to settle his thoughts. 'He's trying to deal with this dispassionately, intellectually,' he said. 'That was my mistake, at first. But these events were driven by emotions – by passions. We have to use feelings, gut reactions, if we're ever going to understand what really happened.'

TWENTY-FIVE

A nineteenth-century notebook, a dark purplish-blue cover, lightly embossed, a little scuffed at the corners, the spine strengthened with a darker blue strip, smooth, textured like linen. Inside, thin pages, lined, the handwriting elegant, sloping, the upward strokes balancing the downward strokes, the black ink hardly faded, every page filled.

The diary entries were written in the notebook at a bureau in a drawing-room that no longer existed. Nothing left, now, of the modest Georgian house and garden except three of the acacia trees that once sheltered it from the north. Tall old trees, just beginning to lose their leaves and drift into winter sleep and perhaps dream, if trees can dream, of the house they once knew. Or perhaps not. To the trees it had just been a building, taking up space, showing lights for a little while after dark, not so very different from the supermarket that had taken its place – apart from the restless cars prowling in and out of the huge forecourt.

The diary had been read many times over the years, usually silently, in a foreign country. But it didn't speak the language there and was not properly understood. Now certain passages were being read in The Village, close to the place where they were written. Not the passages which described wild birds seen in the garden, meals planned and eaten, family and friends entertained to dinner, but the passages written in distress or high anxiety, the writer taking some comfort from the regular sweep of the pen, the careful construction of the letters, the neat flourish of the loops. Maybe here they would be understood more easily . . .

A mishap at the mill today. There is no need for a shield on the looms if reasonable care is taken. But somehow E.H. became caught and no one could pull him free. Edward closed the mill for the rest of the day out of respect but I fear there will be repercussions. These people are unable to understand that accidents are inevitable. They must accept the work and the risks, or take neither. And in any case, death will come to all of us in our time.

Today it happened. Graham's horse fell and threw him. Edward was forced to shoot the poor beast.

Graham's injuries were more severe than we at first realised. Surely things will not go as far as I now fear.

My son is dead.

I can hardly believe I am writing this, but I half-think she is a witch. Naturally this is not the first time the idea has come into my mind, but it is the first time I have allowed it to stay. No one who offends her seems to go unpunished. I have just heard a new story concerning her. It appears she had hopes of Mr Rogers for her daughter. A foolish conceit since his family is far superior to hers. Yet no sooner did he marry Miss Williams, three years ago, than his fields flooded, his sheep sickened, and within months he was bankrupt and forced to leave his land.

Yesterday I went to see her at Honeysuckle Cottage. A pretty name for an evil place. I had heard he had died and I was afraid.

*I know Edward would be angry if he so much as suspected I
was pleading with such a woman. But I felt obliged to, although
I like to think I kept my dignity. Are her eyes truly strange, or
do I believe they are strange because I am afraid of her? She
came to her door to hear me. We stood in the sunlight. The
honeysuckle was full of bees. I had always liked bees, but these
seemed to me like tiny demons, swarming around their mistress.
I have regretted my visit ever since, and always shall. It was
unpleasant and no use. She had already begun it and would not
be turned from her course.*

*Today she came to me with her view of the future. It frightened
me, as she intended. I suggested she approach Edward. I knew
his only emotions in such a situation would be anger and scorn.
She paid me no heed and simply repeated what she has told me
before, that I must never speak of this, or of her. I cannot believe
I allow her to threaten me, yet it seems that I do. All I can do is
wish her injured or dead so she can no longer terrorise and
manipulate.*

*I think every thing has ended for us here. How can we stay in
the face of such hatred? We saw the smoke and the glow from
the house, and I knew what she'd done. The fire engines were
there before us but there was little they could do. The wind blew
the flames on to the cottages of Church Row and the thatch
caught and all efforts were naturally diverted to try and save
them. It was terrible to see. They were all lost and some of the
cottagers with them. I cannot believe such a cruel end was
intended for those innocent folk. Had the mill stream not been
such a good source for the pumps, I think the Church might
have been lost, also, and the houses on the other side of The
Green. The Chief Fire Officer has told us that never, in all his
experience, has he encountered such a conflagration. I cannot*

105

stop thinking of what I was shown. It seems impossible, yet it is true.

TWENTY–SIX

It was important to tidy up the pictures and the box of paints before going out. It wasn't right to leave them lying scattered on the table, as if they were just pieces of paper and tubes of pigment, as if they had no potency left.

Jan turned each painting the right way up and folded its piece of protective tissue paper over it. She straightened the tubes of paint, and put back the brushes which someone, probably John, had taken out. It wasn't possible to arrange the dead leaves as they should be – too much handling had reduced them to dust, and a lot of the dust had scattered on the table and floor and been swept up by Trish. Jan did the best she could.

Ned reached out and touched the corner of the box, very gently. 'The wood's bruised,' he said. 'I think it was thrown into the attic and I think the pictures were thrown after it.'

A flicker of irritation went through Jan. The box had been touched enough, she wanted it left alone. She dragged it across the table towards her, out of Ned's reach.

'Why would someone throw it?' said Kate.

'Think of it from Isabella's angle. Millie comes and tells her to paint the mill – but to paint it as if it was on fire. And then it actually *does* go on fire. She must have been horrified. If she was as scared of Millie as Jane was, she might not have dared destroy everything, however

much she wanted to. So she did the next best thing –
flung everything into the attic in a panic and had it
boarded up.'

The action of pulling the box across the table had sent
all the paint tubes askew again. Trying to settle them, in
nests made from the few surviving handfuls of dried leaf,
Jan's fingers touched a little tab of cloth.

It lifted easily, bringing with it a piece of card, cut
exactly to fit the bottom of the box. The tubes of paint
began to slide, but Jan raised the card, slowly, higher and
higher. Hidden underneath lay one more picture.

'What have you found?' said Ned, noticing.

Jan took the picture out, closed the box, ignoring the
disarray inside, and put it on the lid where they could all
see it.

'Good grief!' said Ned.

'It's not like the others,' said Kate, in a whisper.

It was as primitive as a cave painting, the people not
much more than pin men sketched in with black paint
against a dark blue background. They were arranged in
pairs, in lines. The pair at the top were the largest. Below
them were three smaller pairs, and so on down the
page, with the lines getting longer and the figures
getting smaller – almost like a family tree. There were
orange stars behind and beside and above them. The
figures could have been dancing against a starry night
sky – or they could have been writhing in pain –
especially as each one was streaked with red paint. A
tiny shred of cloth had been stuck to each figure, and a
little bit of hair had been stuck to each head – faded
hair, real hair, human hair. All around the edge of the
picture was a scalloped pattern that could have been

made with bits of broken seashell, but wasn't.

'What are these?' said Kate, touching the scalloped edges.

'Fingernail parings,' said Ned, softly.

'Yuck!' said Kate, snatching her hand back and wiping it on her skirt.

'Any date on the back?' said Ned.

Jan turned the picture over, holding it carefully by its edges. 'No,' she said. 'Some numbers – like on the other pictures – but no date.' She turned the picture back the right way and put it down again. Her hands were steady, but she was shaking so much inside that she felt as though her bones were dissolving. She looked up at Ned. 'Did Jane write about Isabella in her diary?' she said.

'No,' said Ned. 'I'd have remembered the name.'

'But she does write about Millie Harrison?'

'Well, yes, you heard . . .'

'By name? She uses her name?'

'No, but she wouldn't. She was warned not to speak of her – I assume she was also afraid to write about her. I guess she thought it was OK if she kept it anonymous.'

'So how do you know it was Millie she was afraid of?'

Ned looked at her in silence for a moment. 'Because she talks about a witch living in Honeysuckle Cottage,' he said slowly, 'and Millie Harrison was living in Honeysuckle Cottage at the right time, and people were so sure she was a witch they renamed her house The Witches Cauldron.'

Jan moved away from the table, moved across to the front door, opened it and went out, leaving it wide behind her.

'Jan!' said Kate. 'Where are you going? You can't just walk out!'

Ned didn't say anything. His face set in a curiously blank expression, he followed Jan. Kate, on his heels, was so certain Jan would have gone in the direction of the bonfire, the crowds, the pub, that she stumbled out of the door looking to the right and didn't see her. For a moment it seemed as though Jan had vanished totally.

But Ned knew where to look, because Ned had guessed already. Jan had turned sharp left out of the door and now she was on her knees in front of the house, digging with her hands in the earth close to the wall.

'What are you *doing*?' said Kate, her voice panicky. She was beginning to feel a crushing sense of responsibility. Jan had seemed to be sliding towards some sort of edge for two days, and all she'd done was watch and worry. She wished she'd talked to Mick – or Trish – or anyone.

Ned reached out and touched the wall above Jan's head. In the light from the street lamp it wasn't hard to see that a section of stonework, about six foot by three, was very slightly different from the rest, newer, put in place not more than fifty years ago to block off a front door that was no longer needed, the front door to the original cottage, Isabella's cottage.

Jan sat back on her heels. Her frantic scrabbling had uncovered the remains of an old, gnarled, woody root, not very deep under the earth.

'I wonder what that is,' said Ned. But he wasn't wondering. He knew.

'It's a honeysuckle root,' said Jan.

'*No!*' said Kate. 'No, you can't be sure, it could be anything.'

'It's a honeysuckle,' said Jan. 'I'm certain. This half of the house – the half where Isabella lived – used to be Honeysuckle Cottage. It was Isabella. It was *all* Isabella.' She looked up at them and her eyes were bright with excitement. 'And you know what's really horrible?' she said. 'She didn't just predict those terrible things. She made them happen.'

TWENTY–SEVEN

It had found someone else. Like the last one, but different. The blood and skin smelt the same but there was no bitterness in this one, no raging sense of injustice and hatred to lock into. That was why it hadn't recognised her potential at first. It had tried her out, briefly, a few times, as it had tried out various creatures and objects, and had moved on, believing some inbuilt malevolence was essential. But now it had discovered that this one had another quality, quite different but almost as useful – this one didn't care. She couldn't be bothered to make choices. She wouldn't initiate anything, but she wouldn't oppose it, either.

Also, she wouldn't understand she was being used until it was too late.

The other one had wanted to cause harm, and would willingly and knowingly empower anything that could achieve this (until eventually she lost her nerve and allowed others to shut away her resources, and it with them, leaving it half-sleeping in the darkness for generations.) This one didn't mind about things, or perhaps didn't notice, and that was almost as good. Better, perhaps. The other one had used it. This one would allow it to use her.

There need be no delay. Last time the woman had had to be guided into making the instruments – led to the herbs in the fields and woods – taught the recipes, charms, words and colours in dreams. No need for all that this time. This time everything was ready.

Such pictures there would be! Such powerful pictures!

TWENTY–EIGHT

Back in the house Kate, looking at the latest addition to the weird art show scattered on the table-top, said, 'Shall I find John to come and see it? Shall I find your parents?'

'No,' said Jan.

The light was falling on the picture from two directions – from the street lamp outside the window and from the side lamp on the end of the mantelpiece. Each scrap of cloth and hair and fingernail had its own shadow. The black writhing figures receded into the blue background and the orange stars flared almost as brightly as fireworks. Isabella had used watercolours, but she'd laid the paint on so thickly it had something of the gloss of oil.

'Look at the stars,' said Ned. 'They all have the two points at the top.'

'So?' said Kate.

'A true five-pointed star has the single point at the top,' said Ned. 'Inverted, it's a sign of evil.'

'It's the most dangerous of them all,' said Jan. 'This is to bewitch the whole family. It's a spell to go right down the generations. Think of *making* something like this—!'

Kate looked quickly at her. Was Jan as shocked and disturbed as she was, or was she – could she be – impressed? Kate couldn't tell.

Jan looked down at her hands. The scratch and the splinter marks were bright against the pale skin.

Although it had no eyes or ears, it enjoyed watching and listening as they prepared to reconstruct the story, getting it right at last, with only a few details missing.

It was confident the girl was well under control now – the horrid fascination had caught her.

Kate, who was standing with her back to the stairs, was suddenly very aware that the light from the room only reached halfway up them. Above was darkness, and the ladder connecting the landing with the gaping opening above it. She turned sharply and looked over her shoulder. 'I wish your Dad had shut the attic again,' she said, 'with this in it.'

This other girl might be a nuisance. It had tried to use her once or twice but hadn't been able to find any kind of foothold. It didn't understand her and decided to ignore her.

The boy was different. His thin, pale hands with the signet ring had stirred a faint memory of other hands – hands of long ago, hands belonging to a man called Edward Meredith, a man who had made money from a textile mill that exploited and maimed and killed; a man whose hands had touched every young female worker, and whose hectoring voice had demanded compliance and silence on pain of dismissal.

It had been amused to discover that Isabella had not totally gone. Humans think they bury or burn their dead, but they only bury or burn the body that died, not the particles it shed over the years, not the memory. It didn't even have to create a new resentment. Isabella's dust still held its hatred, its obsessional hatred, for Edward Meredith. And the dust and the memory had been woken by the arrival of this boy, this Meredith descendant. If it could have felt warmth it would have felt warmth towards young Ned Meredith, but it could not. Nor did it care that he was unlikely to survive this.

They all three paid more attention now, to the diary, to the pictures, to the numbers on their backs. Ned cracked the code – so quickly he was cross with himself for not trying sooner. 'It's letters for numbers,' he said, 'The simplest of them all. She must have relied on no one bothering.'

'She was right to, wasn't she?' said Jan.

Ned pulled a felt-tip pen out of his pocket and printed the letters of the alphabet across the edge of the newspaper, below the article on Fires and the Dead, and numbered each, from one to twenty-six. Then he transliterated the numbers into words.

To Flood, announced the numbers on the back of the field with its submerged fence; To Fall, on the horse throwing its rider; To Rot, on the kneeling sheep; To Break, on the milk wagon with its cracked wheel; To Burn, on the blazing mill. And on the final picture, encrusted with nails and shreds of cloth and hair – To Curse.

It was Kate who fetched the painting of The Witches Cauldron from the wall, and Kate who noticed that the creeper all over it wasn't honeysuckle but ivy, its little three-pointed leaves quite easy to identify where a tendril drooped over the doorway.

It was Kate who saw something else, too. She was tipping the frame this way and that, trying to get light on the picture without getting reflection on the glass. Suddenly she made a sharp little sound and almost dropped it onto the table.

'What?' said Jan.

'You have to look really carefully,' said Kate. 'On the windowpanes. See? Tiny stars, very faint. Upside down.'

Ned slid the picture from its frame and read out the numbers on the back. '20, 15, space, 2, 12, 1, 13, 5. To Blame. Isabella shifted it all on to Millie.'

'Poor Millie,' said Kate. 'Mrs North was right, it shouldn't be called The Witches Cauldron. She didn't do anything . . .'

'She did something,' said Jan, her voice unusually harsh. 'She must have been in on it too, she must have helped Isabella.'

'How do you mean?'

'All the cloth and hair and fingernails —,' said Jan. 'How would Isabella have got those? Millie must have collected them when she worked in the Meredith's house. It must have taken her months . . .'

'Millie had her own reason to hate us,' Ned said quietly. 'Her brother was killed by the mill machinery.'

They read the diary again, sitting hunched together at the end of the table.

'Keep substituting Isabella for Millie,' said Ned, 'and it all comes out differently. It was Isabella who wanted the farmer, Mr Rogers, to marry her daughter. It was Isabella who threatened him when he married Miss Williams instead — and flooded his fields and made his sheep ill.'

'And when Jane went to Honeysuckle Cottage,' said Kate, 'she came here.'

'Right there!' said Ned, pointing at the wall beside the sitting room window. 'That's where the door's been sealed off.'

Jan leant back from the table and looked at the place

where Jane had stood, plagued by bees and anxieties, as she had pleaded with Isabella not to carry out whatever threat it was she had made. Her expression was unreadable.

'And this was Isabella's parlour,' said Kate in a whisper. '*This* room – here – where we are . . .'

'When Jane wrote about calling here because someone had died –,' said Ned, trying to turn the fragile pages gently, 'where is it – here – this bit, where she says, . . . *I went to see her at Honeysuckle Cottage. A pretty name for an evil place. I had heard he had died and I was afraid . . .* We thought the 'he' who had died must be Millie Harrison's brother Elias. But it wasn't. That had happened much earlier – Jane writes about E. H. and the accident with the machinery way back. *This* death was someone else – someone belonging to Isabella—'

'The one John said about just now?' said Kate. 'The one who only had a small injury but then got gangrene or something?'

'I guess so. I wonder if there's some way to find out who it was . . . not that it matters, now, this long after . . .'

Jan listened, but said nothing. She sat quietly, a little apart from the other two now. She spread her hands out on the table and looked down at them, wondering if they looked like Isabella's hands. She turned them over and examined the palms. As far as she knew, there weren't any pictures of Isabella. She would never know if she was like her, if her hands were the same shape, the fingers the same length, perhaps even the same network of lines lying across the palms . . .

'But if Millie helped Isabella,' Kate was saying – 'getting those . . .' she gave a slight involuntary shudder – '. . .

those fingernails and stuff, that means they *must* have been friends. But Jan's Grandpa remembers them and *he* said they weren't.'

'They fell out,' said Ned. 'Work it back. Remember the woman in the library? What's she called?'

'Mrs North.'

'Right, Mrs North. Remember how she said her grandfather was saved from the fire as a baby – the only survivor when the cottages burned? Then remember what John said. Mrs North is descended from Millie Harrison's niece. It has to have been Millie's niece – and almost her whole family – who died in those cottages. When Isabella torched that mill, the fire got out of hand and there were all those deaths, and Millie couldn't forgive her . . .'

Jan, gazing around the table, saw that Ned's pen was lying just within reach. She reached out and picked it up and held it, like a paintbrush, wondering how it had felt to be able to make things happen . . .

Carefully, slowly, she printed a series of numbers across the back of her left hand. 20 15 2 21 18 14, she printed, whispering the numbers to herself as she wrote them. Then she whispered the words they stood for. 'To Burn.'

'What are you doing?' said Kate, noticing.

'I'm her descendent,' said Jan, calm now, agitation gone, tears dry. 'I wondered if I might have inherited her powers. I wondered if I could use the paints the way she did. I just thought I might try . . .'

Yes, it told her, in her thoughts. Yes. You can. You can do it. Go on, go on, go on.

TWENTY–NINE

'Oh . . . no . . . Jan!' said Kate, staring down at the numbers, which had blurred slightly on the back of Jan's hand.

'I don't think this is such a great idea,' said Ned.

Jan found it surprisingly easy to unscrew the lids from the tubes. She had imagined that they might be stuck tight with ancient paint, but they weren't, and the pigment inside was still moist. It gave off a very faint, strange smell and, for a moment, it seemed almost luminous.

She squeezed paint directly on to the bristles of the smallest brush, and spread it carefully on the palm of her hand to make a brown shape that could have been a bonfire, then a splash of red near the bottom that could have been a flame.

'Jan, no!' said Kate, firmly this time, with conviction. She caught at Jan's wrist. 'Wash it off – don't do it – it might be dangerous – we need to think about this.'

Jan snatched her arm free and then leant forward to whisper right in Kate's face. 'You're just jealous,' she hissed, and her eyes were hard and blank, her face distorted with a mixture of contempt and unhealthy pleasure. 'You're jealous because I'm the one doing things now, not you. I'm in the centre, not you.'

Shaken, hurt and silenced, Kate stepped back.

It was exultant. That was Kate done for. Kate

would not be a problem after that.

'We'll go outside now,' said Jan, dreamily. She had to open the door with her left hand – holding her right hand carefully, palm flat, fingers spread, so as not to smudge the sticky paint.

Kate turned to Ned. 'What do we do?'

'We stick with her,' said Ned. 'It may be OK. Maybe all those things happened by chance. But we stick with her.'

Cars were parked nose to tail around The Green, and the shifting crowd near the unlit bonfire at the other end was huge, much denser than they had expected. The murmur of numerous people talking to each other made a steady humming sound. Impossible to recognise anyone, muffled up as they were against the cold, especially as the glow from the street lamps didn't quite reach that far, and nor did the circle of light blazing out from the windows and open door of The Weaver's Arms. Easy to see the pub was full, people were overflowing on to the forecourt in front.

'Wow!' said Ned.

'The whole world's here!' said Kate.

'Watch,' said Jan. She crossed the road onto the grass. Then she stood still, half the length of The Green away from her target, and held up her right hand in a gesture that looked almost like a blessing.

As the crowds milled to and fro, gaps opened and closed between them, revealing glimpses of the great pile of wood.

They all three saw the flame at the same moment, low down, near the base of the structure.

'See?' said Jan.

'They've lit the fire, that's all!' said Kate, panic in her voice. 'It's time and they've lit it.'

But as the flame grew, the steady humming sound was joined by one or two voices shouting. Then four figures ran out of the pub, Harry the landlord, George the newsagent, Mr Walsh and Jason. As they ran, determined not to be cheated of the ceremonial lighting, they were hastily setting matches to the torches that had been carefully prepared, to await Harry's signal.

The people gathered near the door of the pub pulled back to let them through, and – running faster now – they just had time to make a circle around the bonfire and throw their flaming torches into it before the flames that were already burning could take proper hold.

'They didn't light it,' said Jan. 'We lit it. Me and Isabella.'

THIRTY

Isabella's flame and the fire from the burning torches ate into the pile of wood, crackling and flaring up its sloping sides and into its heart. The crowd cheered and pushed forward, then pulled back a little as they felt the heat and saw the spark-clusters rise and glitter and die against the black sky. The reflection of the bonfire glimmered in the window-panes of the nearest cottages. The smoke flowed gently upwards, steady, unwavering, on the still air.

Jan watched, dazzled – and not only by the flickering light. It had worked perfectly. It was really hers. The power to make things happen. It was so easy. It wasn't even necessary to paint well. All that was required was to concentrate on the target while she worked, and to focus her mind by writing the spell, in Isabella's code.

Until that moment she hadn't thought what she would use it for. Yet now, extraordinarily, she found she already knew. As well as the excitement of her legacy she was feeling something else. There was anger, resentment, a bitterness that seemed to be outside her and inside her at the same time. Oddly, it seemed to be connected with Ned.

It came into her mind that, now, she could punish whoever she chose, whenever she chose. No one would stop her, because no one would know how it was done. Even if she used Isabella's paints to commit crimes, and even if she confessed to the crimes, no one would believe

123

her – so they would allow her to remain free, they would let her go on.

Even if they did become suspicious, and decided to check up on her, they would only discover she had been at home at the time of whatever tragedy they were investigating – at home with her parents, quietly occupying herself with watercolours. Such an innocent hobby, they would say, not much talent, but how nice she's creating something and not just watching television – and how nice that it's a family thing, an interest inherited from her own great-great-grandmother.

It was dancing in her now – made vigorous by all the energy it had been absorbing for days and by the violent erratic rage it had found and woken in Isabella's dust.

Jan pushed through the crowds and moved closer to the fire, her fire. Cal and his cohorts would never be a problem again. What should she choose? A painting of a car smash, perhaps. No survivors. Or would horrific and disabling injuries be more satisfying?

If Gina became too arrogant, some facial disfigurement would soon humble her.

And Ned himself! Ned had survived the bike crash and coughed his lungs clear of the choking dust, but next time he wouldn't be so fortunate. Next time he and those hands of his, those too-familiar hands, so well remembered, still so hateful, would be destroyed – because destruction is the only thing that is final, destruction brings peace. Until the next time.

Why did she hate Ned so much? She couldn't remember. She had thought she liked him – but something in her wanted to finish him, and it was very strong.

She was vaguely aware that Ned was talking to her. He was on one side of her and Kate on the other, close, crowding in on her, as if they were trying to shelter her from something. They were both talking, now she thought about it, but somehow she couldn't understand their words.

The people shifting and mingling around the bonfire looked like strangers – yet why should she expect to recognise them anyway, in the half-dark and the firelight, collars turned up, faces shadowed by scarves and hats, heads mostly turned away from her towards the place where the flames climbed Isabella's broken staircase to caper and feast on ragged cardboard and splintered wood.

So many people on The Green now – not all of them circling the fire – some just standing in groups, looking in her direction. More were arriving, on silent feet, not speaking, the women in long skirts, the men in dark cloth trousers and heavy jackets, children hiding behind them, peering at her past them. They seemed less substantial, yet more important, than the rest.

A couple seemed to come out of the Walshes cottage, but they were not the Walshes. Several were making their way across from the Memorial Gardens. They were partly hidden by the chestnut tree, whose huge shadow was leaping to the rhythm of the flames, men and women, old and young, some carrying babies, others leading tiny children by the hand. The shadow created a strange effect – the illusion of a row of small cottages where really there was nothing but grass and evergreen shrubs.

The mobiles in the window of The Witches Cauldron drifted gently in circles, as though the air had moved softly near them. A patch of darkness beside the door became the figure of a woman, a cat in her arms, approaching more closely than any.

'Look!' said Jan, pushing Kate to make her turn and look and see. Kate did turn but all she said was, 'What? What is it?' Kate could turn and look, but she couldn't see.

'Someone coming out of that cottage . . .'

'What are you talking about . . .?'

'I can do anything,' said Jan, her voice flat, expressionless. 'Any horrible thing I want.'

'But you don't want to do horrible things,' said Kate urgently.

'I won't be able to help it,' said Jan. 'It's my inheritance. I can't help that.'

'You can!' said Kate. 'Of course you can. What you do is *your* choice!'

Jan felt as though something was moving through her blood and her bones, shaking her to get her attention. Fetch the paints, it was saying, go on, you know how. Start with Cal, it doesn't matter that he isn't here, it'll work. Do the first one now, get it out of the way, why not – later there'll be others – so many others.

The woman who had come out of the cottage, the cottage that would one day become the Witches Cauldron Gift Shop, was right beside her now, her face in shadow. She dropped the cat gently on to the ground at Jan's feet.

'Get her away from me!' said Jan.

But no, she had misunderstood, it had not been the woman's voice she had been hearing in her head, it had been something else, something unrecognisable, something not human.

The woman was speaking to her now. Her mouth didn't move, and her outline was fading, but her words were clear – *A son for a son, Isabella*, she was saying. *You took a son for a son . . .*

Jan's own voice was a whisper. 'Who are you? Why are you calling me Isabella . . .?'

What good did it do? came the silent words. *What good could that ever do? And then all those others—*

'Millie?' said Jan – but the woman seemed to have slipped away.

After her voice – soft, full of grief – the other voice, the one that was growing stronger each time it spoke, sounded vicious, heartless . . . Almost demonic.

The world seemed to be shifting, tipping. Too many shadows. Too many people, closing in, looking at her sorrowfully. The night of fires and the dead. The fire was lit, the dead were here.

And still those words, too deep inside her to shut out – use the paints, they're yours, you always knew they were yours, and the power is all yours too, you know it is.

'Kate!' said Jan, 'I'm scared!' And suddenly her voice was normal, like her own self, but younger – childish – afraid –

'It's OK,' said Kate, clinging onto her arm as if to prevent her from floating away. 'I'm here.'

'But I've been so nasty to you.'

'You're allowed to be nasty to friends. I'll help you . . . what do you want me to do?'

It had not allowed for this. It had not been able to read Kate so it had not understood that she might be an obstacle. It needed to separate the two. It didn't have time to work on her again, to search for something nasty or spiteful or negative to lock into, but it could try a simple trick. It could manipulate a positive emotion.

'Millie Harrison's here,' said Jan, looking around, not able to see the shadowy woman any more, 'I think they're all here . . .'

It sensed the concern flowing out of Kate, caught at it, sent a message sliding backwards along the waves of affection and anxiety – go for help, said the message. Go now. Go.

Kate stared at Jan. Then, 'I'm going to fetch your parents,' she said, and the next second she was gone, in among the crowd. She could only see half the people who were gathered on The Green, she could only see the ones who were still alive, but there were easily two hundred of them. She found Gina, found Jason, found her own father, but she was unable, among the shifting mass, to find either of the two she really needed.

'I wanted her to stay with me,' said Jan, bleakly.

'It's OK,' said Ned, touching her arm. 'I'm still here – I'll help you.'

It started to sing in her blood once more – she's gone – she'd have stopped you – you're free now – you know what to do – you know how – you know you can paint on anything – your hand, a lamp-post, the pavement, the trunk of the tree – no blame – not your fault – so quick – so easy – you can put an end to him.

'No! Ned you can't help! Get away! Keep away from me! It hates you!'

'What hates me?'

'I don't know,' said Jan, 'but it's strong – it's really, really strong.' She pushed him away from her, hard, and ran, dodging through the parked cars, back to the double cottage, back to Honeysuckle Cottage, where the box of paints lay, open and inviting, ready for use.

THIRTY-ONE

The box was as fascinating and as repellent as the white spiders. No, not repellent – tempting. Tempting, but heavy to lift, awkward to carry. Yet she couldn't stay alone indoors with it, she had to take it outside.

Coming out of the front door, crossing to The Green, moving back into the smokey air, the box held flat in her arms, Jan searched for someone to tell her what to do.

It sang to her all the while – you know what to do, you enjoyed lighting the fire, made you feel important, powerful, you can be important and powerful again, whenever you want –

Ned had not seen where she had run to – was still looking for her.

Kate had given up trying to find Trish or Mick, or even John, and had gone instead to The Weaver's Arms where Grandpa Lyle sat, his chair pulled up to the window so he could look out in comfort.

Jan saw the two of them coming out of the pub, Grandpa Lyle slow, Kate holding his arm, trying not to hurry him. She went to meet them.

He found it hard to focus after the brilliant lights inside the pub. The sharp air made his eyes water and the fire reflected in the tears and dazzled him. 'Aren't you cold, love?' he said to Jan. 'Where's your coat?'

Kate, supporting him, looked from one to the other. She had been so desperate to fetch a responsible grown-up that she hadn't known what she expected him to do, only that she'd somehow expected him to take charge, sort everything out. Now for the first time she understood how old he was, how frail, that she should have gone on searching for Jan's parents, screamed out their names until they answered.

It was the first time Jan had been almost-alone with her grandfather since the discovery in the attic. 'Grandpa,' she said, 'Can you remember Isabella?'

He looked fussed, mystified.

'Isabella – your grandmother.'

'I know who she was.'

'What was she like?'

'Bitter.'

'Were you scared of her?'

He shrugged. 'She died when I was very young.'

'But you knew her – you knew she was bitter . . .'

He looked into her eyes, looked at the box she was holding against her chest. 'I think perhaps someone told me that,' he said. 'I think my father told me. She had a hard life, so I heard. My grandfather was a farm labourer – used to be a big farm round here – but they mechanised it – didn't want so many men. He was out of work for the rest of his life. She had to earn the money.'

He looked around him and Kate, realising he was looking in vain for somewhere to sit down, tried to take a little more of his weight on her shoulder, but he was a big man and it wasn't easy.

'He didn't work at the mill?' said Jan.

'No, but she did. Isabella did. And so did their son. He'd have been my uncle. He hurt his arm in a loom – didn't seem bad at first but it went rotten – it was blood poisoning took him off.' He gave a cold little laugh. 'It had to be my grandfather's own son who died,' he said, almost to himself, 'not *his* son. Fate favours the powerful – it wasn't the rich mill-owner's son, it wasn't Meredith's son. His son was only a child when the mill went up in flames.' He shook his head, in a kind of bewilderment. 'Still,' he said, 'in the end I'm glad Meredith's son didn't die.'

'Meredith's son *did* die,' said Kate, cautiously, not sure if he was rambling. 'But not at the mill. He fell off a horse.'

Grandpa Lyle peered down at her as if he might have forgotten who she was. 'That was Meredith's first son, his son by his wife, as died in a riding accident,' he said. 'And his second son by his wife, the one that was still a boy when the mill caught fire, went to Canada with them. I'm talking about one of his other sons and daughters. I'm talking about his son with Isabella.' He rubbed one hand across his watery eyes. 'I'm talking about my father.'

Jan couldn't speak. She drew her breath in and then couldn't let it out again. She felt she was drowning in air.

Then Kate said, very softly, 'I don't believe it,' though it was obvious that she did, and Jan got control of her breath again and said, 'Your father was a Meredith? We're Merediths?'

'There's more Merediths in this village than have ever been called that,' said Grandpa Lyle. 'Didn't I tell you, Trish? I thought I told you when you were twenty-one.'

'I'm not Trish,' said Jan. 'Grandpa – I'm her daughter.'

'It's not important – it's all over and gone – keep the attic closed. My father put a stop to her. She could hate almost all Merediths, but she couldn't hate her own baby, no more'n I could hate my own Dad. We never thought of him as a Meredith – he was called a Lyle – like my grandfather – like me. When he was grown and she was gone, he locked it all away.' He frowned at the box in Jan's arms, as though he found it hard to focus. 'What are you going to do with that?'

'She's not going to do anything,' said Kate fiercely. 'Are you?'

'Yes,' said Jan. 'I have to. I can't help it.'

'You can!' said Kate. 'You're a free person. What you do is *your* choice!'

'It's all best forgotten,' said Grandpa Lyle. 'Can I go home now? I'm tired.'

'Come on,' said Kate. She turned him gently, aiming for the pub because it was closer than the cottage. She looked over her shoulder at Jan. 'Come with us,' she said, as firmly as she could. 'Come on. Your parents'll be along to fetch him soon.'

Jan shook her head. She stood where she was and let them go, Grandpa Lyle leaning on Kate, both of them moving away from her, pushing through the unconcerned crowds. Kate called back over her shoulder, her words cutting through the blur of other sounds – 'It's *your* choice!' She shouted it twice.

Jan turned away and walked across the dark grass, clumsy because of the heavy box in her arms – bumping into some people – moving right through others – until she was standing where she wanted to be.

She knelt, set the box down on the grass, and raised the lid.

Too much to think about, too much to try to understand – but one thing was sure. Here, in the paints, was power, more power than she had ever imagined. Using was power, choosing was power, and that power was hers. No one else could do this. Only she, with Isabella's blood in her veins and Isabella's dust under her fingernails. It was hers, uniquely hers.

Slowly, she unscrewed the cap on each old lead tube of colour.

The flames wandered over the surface of the bonfire – outlined against the sky like scarlet feathers – but the heart of the fire was a furnace now, dark red and fierce, shimmering the air with waves of heat. The heat stung Jan's face, made her eyes feel dry and gritty.

With a sound like distant gunfire, the display in Central Gardens exploded into the sky in showers of jewels that burst through each other in ever widening rings. Everyone else turned and looked up, everyone else stared, topaz and ruby and sapphire and emerald stars were reflected in almost every eye.

Jan picked up the box and stood, holding it in both hands. It was closed, now, though it would no longer lock because it was too full. Inside, on top of the paint, which she had squeezed out of the tubes, and the empty tubes themselves, and the brushes, and the crumbled leaves, was a picture of other stars against another sky, figures stabbed with gashes of red, hair and nails and cloth to identify them, to mark them out as victims of a charm whose potency could flow down the years but could not cross a great ocean.

She stood sideways to the fire, swung the box away from it and then flung it with all her strength, towards the blazing centre.

It was heavier than she'd thought, it didn't arch

through the air as she'd expected, it didn't reach her target. It landed at the very edge, in embers and ashes, at the point where Isabella's flame had first taken hold. It lay at an angle, the lid slightly open, leaf dust dribbling out. The power of the fire was surging upwards, away from it. Jan looked wildly around for anything she could use to push it further in. There was nothing.

In her mind she was humming, silently, continuously, to shut out the messages that were crackling through her veins – Get it back, it said, not too late – snatch it quickly – you won't be burned – it isn't damaged – it's all there – it's your present from the past—

A tiny flame wandered towards the box, touched it and retreated. Then it came upon a handful of dead powdery leaves, flared briefly, closed in on the box again – and seemed to attract another flame, and another, and another. The charcoal the box was leaning on gave under its weight and let it fall a little. The flames began to slither over it, sliding on its surface as if they were playing with it, or as if they couldn't get any kind of a purchase on it.

That was when Ned found her. While the distant display rose and fell above the rooftops, claiming almost everyone's attention, he saw her and ran over to her. 'Where did you get to?' he said. 'I've been looking everywhere . . .'

She ignored him and he followed the line of her eyes and saw. 'You're burning it!' he said. He put his arm round her and held her tightly against his side. 'We should have done it at once!' he said. 'Everything'll be OK now.'

The flames sank their claws into the wood with cat-like suddenness and fed, and grew, and changed colour, and all at once the box was burning strongly with green and purple fire. A high, whining, scream came hissing out of it. The flames bunched themselves in a spinning ball of light and then instantly unravelled into a thick snake of vivid flame that lashed out like a whip and wrapped itself around Ned. He flung Jan away from him and fell to the ground, encased in fire.

Jan landed on her hands and knees, and rolled clear, and sat up, all in one movement. She saw Jim running, dragging off his coat, and then he was beside Ned, throwing it over him, wrapping him in it, shouting for help.

Jan struggled to her feet and stood, swaying slightly, rocked by the people running past her from all directions – faces blurred with fear and touched with firelight. She felt something draining away from her, like poison from a wound – and with it was going strength, energy, the ability to see, the ability to hear. Then Kate was there, Trish was near, Mick was at her side and caught her as she almost fainted.

They made her kneel on the damp ground, her head so low the blades of grass stroked her forehead, and gradually the strength flowed back. She stood up carefully, Kate on one side and her father on the other, and now her eyes could focus again, she could hear the voices cutting across each other: What happened? . . . No idea . . . Apparently he's a Meredith . . . fancy him being here for the first fire since . . . is that what you call synchronicity? . . . How incredible he's the one who got burned . . . you could say it's natural justice . . . rubbish, the poor lad's not responsible for his ancestors . . . can't bear grudges forever . . .

'Is he all right,' Jan kept saying, 'is he all right?' No one had an answer for her.

The last of the multi-coloured lights from Central Gardens fell down the sky, died away and were replaced by a blue light, sweeping rhythmically across The Green. Within moments, the paramedics were lifting Ned carefully into the ambulance.

'Dad!' Kate yelled. 'Dad – is he OK?'

Jim got to his feet and worked his way through the crowds towards her. 'He's alive,' he said. 'Burnt and shocked but alive. Did anyone see what happened?'

Jan, unaware that tears were pouring down her face, opened her mouth to speak, but Kate clamped her arm around her shoulders and began to pull her away. 'She needs to go home,' she said firmly, 'Come on, Jan. Don't talk out here.'

Mick agreed with Kate, and the two of them led her back to the cottage, while Trish ran to the pub to fetch Grandpa Lyle.

The party continued on The Green after a fashion. The children had a good time, but no one lit the fireworks and the adults were subdued although, strangely enough, most of them felt a strong sense of relief, which none of them could explain or understand.

The people who hadn't really been there were there no longer – and something unseen shimmered away across the rooftops. It blotted out a star for a brief moment and then was gone, leaving the last fragments of Isabella's dust to sink back into the hidden places where the sleeping memories lay.

THIRTY-TWO

Jan told the true story only to Kate and her distant cousin Ned, both of whom knew most of it already, to her parents and grandfather, and to John. Out of all of them, John was the only one who didn't believe it.

John completed the museum-display on The Fire with Isabella's painting. He also accepted the gift of Edward Meredith's signet ring and exhibited it next to the photograph where it showed so clearly, on the hand that rested on Jane Merediths' shoulder. He was polite about the loss of the box of paints and of what he suspected had been the most interesting picture of them all. He listened quietly to Jan's explanation, and offered no judgement.

Grandpa Lyle understood that the surviving pictures had long since worked their magic and were now harmless, but still declined to have any of them in his sheltered flat. He gave Jan a present, a ring set with a black opal. He explained that it had been her Grandmother's, but it had never had any connection with Isabella.

Ned needed plastic surgery on his hands, and the scarring on the side of his face seemed likely to be permanent, but the prognosis for full recovery was good. His father flew over from Canada to take him home. He met no hostility in the village.

The local paper blamed Ned's accident on a 'rogue firework'. It explained his relationship with Jane and Edward Meredith and lingered on the irony that the first bonfire since The Fire had injured him, and only him. It was happy to report that any bitterness against the Merediths had faded with the passing years, and that numbers of local residents had sent cards and flowers to the hospital. It also published a profile of Jim Summers, Ned's saviour, making much of the fact that he was descended from one of the firefighters who had fought The Fire itself.

Kate gave up trying to suppress the pushy side of her nature. Now she knew Jan couldn't be forced to do anything she didn't want to, it no longer seemed to matter.

The Witches Cauldron continued to thrive. The owners, Mr and Mrs Walsh, saw no reason to change the name. Gina continued to bring her cat to work and to speak in hushed tones of Millie Harrison's dark powers.

The misshapen chestnut tree allowed its last leaves to drift into the churchyard and the Memorial Gardens and then sank into its winter torpor, undisturbed by the brief flurry of flames.

Whatever it was that had shivered away over the rooftops travelled hundreds of miles, or fifty, or perhaps only thirty; blind, cold, relentless – and hunting. But behind the cottage windows, in the spaces under the floorboards, in the cavities between inner and outer walls, up among the roof rafters, the dust settled, and the cottages were at peace.